OBJEKT 221

STEVE METCALF

SEVERED PRESS
HOBART TASMANIA

OBJEKT 221

WWW.SEVEREDPRESS.COM

ISBN: 978-1-925840-83-4

Also By Steve Metcalf

RESET: A Videogame Anecdote
Sketch
The Beast of Trash Island

King Paranormal Investigations Series
Coldwater
The Hidden Riches of Lord Granite
Paradox Iron

Collections
The Event: The Chicago Rust Yards
The Event: Iron Bay
The Event: Precision Robotics

CHAPTER ONE
THE FINAL SPECIMEN

IT SOUNDED like the end of the world. Heavy, thick drops of rain fell in sheets across the landscape, pummeling trees and flattening grass. The air—filled with a palpable dewy sweetness only an hour before—hung as fatly as a gloomy fog as far as the eye could see. Blinding lightning and screaming thunder shook the building to its core.

Jason Beale looked up at the faint line of dust that fell from the ceiling. He could still feel the reverberations of the last blast of thunder as it rattled its way through the building. The sky, black with clouds, had sucked all light out of the building. He reached up and clicked a button on the side of his protective acrylic facemask. He immediately saw the world in night vision—a high-contrast green glow. The corridor lit up in front of him. He turned to look at the rest of the group.

"NVG," he called out over the faceplate's microphone. "Let's keep this shit-show moving."

Nothing had gone right for the advance team all day. From Jacobi clipping a boulder when taking a corner too fast in one of the military-grade LSVs—Light Strike Vehicles—to an equipment failure while trying to catch a bonus specimen on the list, to this ungodly thunderstorm they were now wading through. But they persisted. All 10 men—a combination of field scientists and retired Army Rangers—were crowding through the large corridor at the back of the main floor of Building 5. Beale was in charge of this force as he started counting off names and pointing. Two soldiers per scientist except for Beale's own group.

They had run down the list that intelligence had prepared. As of today's hunting migratory patterns, they were likely to find a specimen in Building 5.

"Roscoe. Halverson. Tenna. You're with me." He stood off to one side. "We go north. Smith. Wilson. Jacobi. You're east. The rest of you take the west branch. We only need one more NR-401G for the lab. Any other specimens can be subdued or eliminated." He hefted the shoulder strap of his Mossberg 500 shotgun—the Persuader—off his right arm. "Quiet if possible." He grinned. "Loud if not."

"Hoorah," the other five soldiers called back as the three teams split apart.

* *

"Do you know the history of that bit of military slang?" Halverson asked. He was dressed in similar camouflage to the two soldiers in his group, but he held a motion detector in one hand and a waterproof computer tablet in the other.

"No, sir, I do not."

Beale was the point man of the group, his shotgun held at eye level. Just behind him were the two scientists, Halverson and Tenna. They were both carrying sophisticated tracking equipment. Tenna had what looked like an electronic checklist blinking away, clipped to his utility belt. They all wore the futuristic-looking acrylic faceplate which had a small soda-can-sized air canister attached to the underside.

Roscoe, a tall man of 25, brought up the rear. He was carrying a Belgian-made FN FAL battle rifle. Many on the team preferred this weapon, or its British variant. He held the rifle in the same manner as Beale held the shotgun but was sweeping his eyesight back and forth in the middle distance of the huge corridor. Roscoe was on high alert, unblinking and staring into the green gloom.

"Radio operators in World War II," continued Halverson without taking his eyes off the motion detector, "shortened the response Heard Understood Acknowledged to HUA. When spoken, it sounded like hooah."

"Fascinating," Beale said, checking his watch. "Six more hours of air."

"Oh, that's not all," Halverson said. "Airborne Rangers adopted the acronym into one of their own. HOOA. Hooah. Head Out Of Ass."

"Shocking," Beale said.

"It caught on from there," Halverson said.

There was no additional response from Beale as they reached the first doorway on the left. The doorways were larger than expected and it always gave Beale pause. He wasn't paid to break down the mysterious findings of the advance team—it was his job to deliver them home safe and secure. Right now, he had a bad feeling about Building 5.

"Entering courtyard," Beale said into his faceplate mic to the entire team.

* *

"Entering courtyard," came Beale's voice over Smith's earpiece. He and Jacobi were escorting their assigned scientist—Wilson—through the east branch of the main corridor. Wilson was carrying a thermal imager while the two soldiers carried weapons—FN FALs to match Roscoe. On his back, Jacobi carried a large, collapsible trap. It would expand to a six by six cube that could be slightly modified to reduce the dimensions as the combination of high-tensile steel and PVC piping was designed to telescope in on itself.

"Copy that," Smith responded. "Leapfrogging rooms along the east hall. Stand by."

* *

There was no update from Harrison, Baker, and Leafly in the west corridor.

* *

The courtyard of Building 5 was immense. It seemed like a multi-purpose room with a stage on one side, a set of stone bleachers on the other, and numerous structures that defied definition. The room was dominated by a series of sculptures along the north wall. The largest one, nearly filling the space from stone floor to curved ceiling, was a tree that was carved to resemble a woman. Her features were blurred and out of proportion. She looked like the 3D representation of an impressionist's painting. All the right pieces were in all the right places but the proportions seemed somehow…wrong.

Beale entered the room first, the big Mossberg held at the ready. Roscoe kept the two scientists in the corridor for a moment. He was swinging his battle rifle first down one path followed by the other. For his part, Halverson held a motion detector through the doorway into the courtyard. It was picking up Beale and nothing else.

While there was only one effective entrance into the room, there were dozens of places to hide. Beale was clearing as many of them as possible and finally motioned for the rest of the team to come into the giant 100 meter by 100 meter room.

Halverson, gently sweeping the motion detector back and forth, walked into the room. As he aimed the unit at the far right corner of the courtyard, he caught a small blip of activity and then nothing. The screen faded back to its default light purple.

"There was, uh," the researcher said, sweeping the small black box back and forth, trying to catch a glimpse of what had triggered the electronic response. "There was some movement over *there*."

Beale turned to look at Halverson, who indicated the corner of the room.

"NVG off," Beale said and clicked on a powerful flashlight attached to the side of his shotgun. The strong beam penetrated the gloomy darkness caused by the thick clouds outside. He slowly swept the beam around the area Halverson had indicated. It was a tangle of branches of varying thickness. It looked like a nest. Ten meters above ground.

"What the—?"

And then it jumped.

* *

Blood.

In the west corridor, the three team members had been literally torn to shreds. The screen of a motion detector was covered in gore, but the warning klaxons were still audible. Suddenly, however, the insistent beeping halted.

Whatever had killed these men had slithered out of range of the tiny machine.

* *

Smith cleared room number four along the east corridor. He and his team were making quick work of their section of Building 5. Unfortunately, they were having no luck finding the specimen that had led them here.

He activated the advance team's chat by simply speaking.

"Beale, come in."

He heard static and then a clipped reply.

"Stand by," Beale said over the radio.

His voice was calm and cool, but there was something behind it. Something screaming. And then gunfire.

The three men ran down the corridor to the Y-junction that would lead them to the courtyard.

* *

Specimen NR-401G dropped from its nest and landed gracefully in front of the team. It immediately skittered to the right and tried to find an exit.

While muted in the night vision filter, the team knew that this specimen was colored a deep brown with dark green stripes. In the natural light, amplified by Beale's flashlight, they could see it a bit more clearly. It was nearly three feet tall and had a tail that seemed too short—just over a foot and a half long—that started the entire width of its body and quickly tapered to a sharp point. No one had yet observed NR-401G using its tail as a weapon, but it seemed more an obvious use than one of balance. The specimen had a long snout full of razor-sharp teeth and what looked like a Mohawk of thick brown bristles from between his eyes halfway down his long neck.

"Stand by," Beale said into his faceplate.

With a quick look left and right, the specimen lunged at Beale who fired his shotgun into the ground to halt the giant lizard's approach. Halverson yelped. Roscoe muscled around the scientist and hurled the protective cage toward the beast.

Four things seemed to happen all at once. First, Roscoe hit the red button on the small black remote attached to the combat webbing across his chest. Second, now activated, a blue laser beam shot out of the control surface of the containment pod as it hurled toward the specimen. Third, the specimen halted, frightened by the gunfire. It had no frame of reference for weaponry, but the sound was scary enough. Fourth, the containment field automatically expanded along its telescoping pipes and fully engulfed NR-401G. It slowly clacked back into place coming to rest on the floor of the courtyard.

Five seconds from start to finish.

It took 20 more seconds for Smith and his team to arrive at the courtyard. By then, NR-401G was sedated after receiving a carefully dosed vapor from Halverson.

"You got him?" Smith asked, holstering his sidearm.

"Yeah." Beale nodded and pointed to the nest up in the corner of the room.

"Shit," Smith said. "When did they start doing *that*?"

Beale shrugged.

"Not sure," he said. "Gonna have to remember that one, though." He turned to the three scientists—Halverson, Tenna, and Wilson—who were standing around the collapsible containment box. NR-401G seemed to be sleeping peacefully. Occasionally, its tail would thump against the reinforced PVC. "Send it home."

Halverson nodded and hit a few buttons on the rear control surface of the unit. Outside, a red light started blinking on one of the LSVs. Inside Building 5, dozens of bearings snapped into place on the bottom of the containment unit and the whole thing started sliding through the courtyard along its mapped path back to the waiting vehicle.

Led by Beale, everyone reached up and snapped their masks back into night-vision mode.

"Anything else?" he asked the group. He gave the question a few seconds of silent response. "Okay. You three," he said, nodding to the three researchers who still huddled together as the containment pod left the room, turned right, and headed down the hallway. "Go with the specimen. Get it secured in an LSV. And you get locked down also. We don't want any more surprises. Jacobi, you're with them."

"Hoorah."

"Roscoe, Smith," Beale continued. "You're with me. We're going to locate Harrison's team and evac double-quick. This building has some bad mojo right now."

* *

The team of Army Rangers made it back to the Y-junction and turned left to follow the path laid out in Harrison's original orders. Both the soldiers and the scientists were maintaining radio silence with only Roscoe trying to raise the west team every 30 seconds or so.

They slowed at the top of the corridor. Each of the three soldiers had activated NVG with a detailed HUD (heads-up display) overlay. They were getting real-time readings of their environment. Temperature. Distance measured by their reticule. It was a line of data along the right side of their vision.

"Harrison, Baker, come in," Roscoe said quietly. The high-tuned microphone in the faceplate could easily pick up his whisper and transmit it over the HD radio signal. There was no answer.

Smith hefted his left arm. Like all of the soldiers, he had what amounted to a laptop computer strapped to his forearm. Roughly the size of a large smartphone, the unit was the epitome of military strategy. He hit a command and the screen came to life. It was both a motion sensor and an overlay of their current location. It was reading the two missing soldiers' units. They were further down the hallway. Not moving.

"I don't like this," Smith said.

Beale nodded.

"Move out," he said.

They had negotiated just more than half of the west corridor and Beale, in the lead, stopped. He held up his right hand in a fist as a wordless signal to the two men behind him to halt. All three took a knee, battle rifles up, eyes forward. Three meters ahead, there was a huge pool of blood, some weapons, a couple pieces of equipment.

And some limbs.

Even worse than that was how the smear trailed off to the right into an open doorway on the north side of the corridor. All three men were stone quiet. Beale crouch-walked to the leading edge of the door. He was careful not to step on the gloved hand that rested on the grime-covered floor.

When he reached the door, he stopped and slowly reached his left hand around to a pocket at his lower back. He pulled out a small rubber ball and gently rolled it around the frame and into the room. The rubber surface of the ball was nearly completely silent and Beale only rolled it far enough to clear the door frame. The ball stopped automatically and started sending a signal back to the three men in the hallway.

On their visors, it resembled a picture-in-picture screen. It was a fairly standard room type on floor one of Building 5. It was about eight meters square with no windows and no furniture. The camera in the small ball's sensor had centered on an object moving, only slightly in the far corner of the room. It was completely in the shadows.

"What the fuck," Roscoe whispered.

Either by hearing this utterance or sensing the three men in the corridor 10 meters away, the creature turned.

"Oh shit," Smith whispered.

They were looking at an uncategorized apex predator. The word "UNCLASSIFIED" was blinking on their faceplate HUD screens with numbers and data flashing all around the image perimeter. Soon, the word was replaced by the text UC-0104 as the shared computer started building a file on the as-yet unstudied dinosaur.

It was nearly 10 feet tall and had to stoop slightly to stand in the room. It stood on its hind legs and had a thick tail curled around its feet. Massive cords of muscle were clearly visible beneath a spiny, reptilian skin. Twin rows of spikes ran the length of its back and tapered to blend in with the base of the tail.

Two of its four arms were holding the lifeless corpse of what was left of the researcher Leafly. Ragged bits of flesh fell from its powerful jaws. It stopped chewing as it turned its head toward the door.

"Barrier," Beale called out as he tossed a flash-bang into the room. He could hear the pop as the tiny canister exploded and the creature roared in anger as it was temporarily blinded. Smith pulled a metal bar out of a thigh pocket and jammed one side into the door frame. He pressed a button and the metal bar instantly expanded to cover the width of the door and then upward as it climbed to the top of the frame. It was instantly attaching itself to the frame with an industrial strength adhesive as Smith and Roscoe were hitting each side of the barrier with nail guns that shot long, spiked projectiles. The door was completely barricaded in 10 seconds. Twelve seconds after Beale had thrown the flash-bang, the barrier shuddered as the creature rammed it with incredible force.

"Gotta go," Beale said.

The three men turned and ran, double-quick, down the corridor to meet up with the scientists and the waiting evac vehicles.

CHAPTER TWO
THE RECRUIT

HER DESK was enormous. The office could have been considered larger-than-average, but the desk as a singular object in the room was simply massive. It was well known around the complex and often commented-on. Not to her face, of course—even though, she probably wouldn't have minded so much.

The desk, they said, had to be fabricated and constructed inside the room because every piece of it was too large to fit through the door.

The desk, they said, required additional concrete and steel girders beneath it so the entire unit didn't collapse the floor.

The desk, they said, weighed 5,000 pounds.

The desk, they said, was responsible for the deaths of 12 men.

Most of the rumors, of course, were perpetuated by the desk's owner—Britta Vragi.

As the operational director of the facility, Objekt 221, Britta worked hard to maintain a professional distance from everyone but her immediate subordinates. She couldn't fraternize with those on her level because there was no one on her level. There were two people above her and a dozen department heads below her.

She was 51 years old and a military veteran. She served in the infantry and her call sign was Mountain. Standing 6'2" and weighing in just over 200 pounds, she was a solid piece of anger that no one wanted to face off against. Now, significantly past her prime, she has lost some of her muscle tone but retained all of the fiery ambition. Britta was built of the sturdiest Nordic stock—her name literally meant "Strength" —and commanded a room with a rare combination of size and intelligence.

The desk, they said, was built to her exacting specifications.

That particular rumor, however, was dead-on true.

She was, right now, sitting at her massive desk, waiting for Miles Lofton whom she had summoned 90 seconds ago.

* *

It was a billion-dollar research facility. Precision Robotics was a multi-national conglomerate that only sought the best of the best in every area possible. When the company selected the type of napkins that would be used in the break room, they held several meetings to discuss numerous factors before the decision was made.

Damon Butcher was the best programmer that Precision Robotics had ever hired—and he didn't even work in the Information Services division. He was a department lead in Theoretical Biometrics and was, right now, working through a turkey sandwich in a small corner of the eighth-floor break room with a co-worker, known only as Jeff.

"Rogue One was on TV last night," Jeff said while munching on a potato chip.

"Oh," Damon said. "Great movie."

"I saw that film in the theater twice and I own the disc. Whenever it's on the tube, I gotta stop and watch."

Damon nodded in response.

"I think there's actually a name for that syndrome. Magnetic Entertainment or something. Plus, it's a little easier to avoid the uncanny valley when you're watching it on the small screen."

Jeff was silent for a moment as he swallowed a bite of sandwich and chased it with a slurp of soda. That action completed, he looked over at Damon.

"What was that?" he asked.

"Which part?" Damon asked. "The Iron Law of Entertainment Attraction or the uncanny valley?"

Jeff pointed at him.

"Yeah. That last one."

"The uncanny valley? You've never heard of this?"

Taking another swig of Coke, Jeff hefted his eyebrows in a "go on" motion.

"All of us tech nerds went nuts when Rogue One came out," Damon said, dabbing the corner of his mouth with a napkin. He paused a moment. "Let me back up. The uncanny valley is a hypothesis that centers on man-made objects imitating life. Essentially, computer graphics and robotics—but it can really refer to anything. You got me?"

"Hanging by a thread."

"Okay," Damon said, folding up his lunch-sized bag of Doritos. "Let's just look at CGI in movies, right? You look at computer graphics in a movie from 15, 20 years ago—like I, Robot—and the boundary between real and CGI is pretty clear. Right?"

"The robots looked nice, but you could always tell they weren't real," Jeff offered with a shrug.

"There you go. Exactly." Damon nodded. "Action movies now blur that line so much more effectively. From creating an entire atmosphere on a green screen to de-aging Robert Downey Jr. in a flashback to removing the crow's feet and loose skin from Tom Cruise's face and neck. Right? It looks more and more real."

"Okay," Jeff said. "Sure."

"So, you have to look at it like a continuum with very blocky, unrealistic graphics on one side and with hyper-realistic you-can't-tell-it-from-a-real-person graphics on the opposite side."

"Sure, technology improves along an exponential spectrum. That's why we have cordless phones."

"Okay," Damon said, narrowing his eyes. "We'll come back to that." He paused for a moment. "Peter Cushing's dead, man. All of those scenes with Grand Moff Tarkin? Computer. They filmed some dude going through the motions and dropped a Peter Cushing skin on him with computers in post-production. You didn't hear about this? It was fairly controversial."

"Maybe. I can't really remember."

"Alright, be that as it may, in the early '70s, Japanese roboticist Masahiro Mori proposed that the more realistic an automaton looked, the more endearing it would become to humans. However, there will be a dip along the continuum. At some point, the realism will be fantastic—but a little...*off*. It will become disturbing. This dip in emotional connection is referred to as the uncanny valley. It represents the point at which technology—computer graphics, in this case—is no longer readily apparent, but some small error or inconsistency causes humans psychological discomfort. Maybe the skin appears too waxy or the hair doesn't flip right in the breeze or the muscle movement under the skin is slightly inconsistent. Whatever. It didn't help, in this case, that everyone knew that Grand Moff Tarkin was dead—and they were watching a computer representation of the man as he would have appeared in 1977."

Damon leaned back in his chair. Reopened the small Dorito bag and closed it again.

"Creepy."

"Exactly," Damon said, leaning forward again. "The crazy thing is that the phenomenon is observed over and over again in various studies.

But there's no clear answer why it happens. Why, at a fairly consistent point, life-like robots or computer-generated people interacting with real people on film make us, collectively, go Eww."

"Hmm," Jeff said, finishing off his lunch and stuffing all of the empty components into a brown paper sack.

"My favorite theory, though, has to do with disease aversion." Damon, likewise, started cleaning up his lunch. It was just about time to get back to the lab.

"Disease aversion?"

"Mm-hm. Sure. Whether it's a function of evolution or simple self-preservation, you avoid someone exhibiting the symptoms of the flu, right? Their skin is flushed. They're sweating. Possibly staggering. Coughing. Rubbing snot on the sleeve of their shirt. You don't get on the elevator with *that* dude. Even on a subconscious level. Maybe you had every intention of getting on the elevator with McSickie but your mind says, *Hey. Take the stairs.* You'll probably justify it to yourself later."

"Okay."

"Think back," Damon said. "In your past. Have you ever met anyone who was missing a finger? Maybe just half a finger? Even before you consciously noticed it and said in your head, *Hmm. Joey doesn't have a pinkie finger on his right hand.* Even before that, your mind has picked up on it and the warning klaxons have started sounding. Something is off about this person. It's not a judgment—they're not better or worse than you because of it—but you've, far below the surface, noticed that there was something off about Joey. Something wrong with him."

"Shit," Jeff said. "Yeah."

Damon nodded.

"See? Take that energy and put it into watching a movie. Consciously, you know that this character is a non-human interacting with all of the real humans. On the surface you know this, but your lizard brain, in the deepest, darkest recesses of your mind, you know. Your subconscious is trying to protect you from this person. *There's something wrong with this guy. Watch yourself.*"

"Damn."

"Yeah," Damon said, grinning. "Pretty cool, right?"

* *

The facility called Objekt 221 contained none of the modern-style flourishes of the global Precision Robotics headquarters. It was function over form. Substance over style. That said, Britta Vragi's office contained one unmissable embellishment—an oil painting of a dinosaur. Vibrant greens and bright oranges framed the image of this enormous green-brown monster staring lovingly at the sunset.

Miles Lofton entered the office and closed the door behind him. He'd had numerous conversations with Britta. Most were professional, but they had often chatted about the latest movie or regional happenstance if they passed in the break room. Even with this familiarity, Britta frightened him a little. Not in the scared-for-your-life sense, but he always felt that he was being judged. Like he could never be honest with her lest his responses would somehow be used against him in the future.

Something ridiculous, like: *"Remember when you mentioned to me that you felt Kraft-branded macaroni and cheese was too cheesy, and you preferred to purchase the generic brands? Well, we're sorry. You're being passed-over for this promotion."*

He strode across the office. Britta, from behind her huge desk, motioned for him to sit down.

"Good afternoo—"

"We need to fill a spot on your team," she said without looking up from an open file folder on her desk. "I've been reviewing your recommendations."

Miles sat forward on the chair. It was a wood-leather amalgamation with mission-style arms and plush black leather pads at the rear and bottom.

"Okay," he said, palms placed flat on his knees.

"Damon Butcher."

The way she said it, Miles wasn't sure if it was a question or statement. Nervous, he started babbling a bit.

"Yes. Sure. Friends for years. Went to school together at Berkeley. He's older. A bit older than me. Thirty-four, I think. He went to the Army before college. Came to school on the GI Bill. Dual degrees. Force Recon."

"That's not a degree." Britta allowed a thin-lipped smile.

"Hah hah. Sure. He was Force Recon in the Army. Didn't talk about it a lot, but he was butt-deep in some mess—as he liked to say. But he obviously can take care of himself. Uh. Um. Degrees in programming and, um, cryptozoology. Went to Stanford for the advanced degree. We talk occasionally on social media. Exchange Christmas cards."

Britta had looked up from the file as Miles was talking. She looked back down, turned a page, closed the whole thing, placed her hands—palms down—on top of it. She looked back at Miles.

"What does he know about our organization?"

"Uh. Okay. Sure," he said. "Only as much as I can say according to our NDAs. He knows the name and that we have many interests. Biological research. High-level overview. Nothing more."

Britta nodded.

"I guess we'll see," she said.

"I can call him, if you'd like."

"Not necessary," Britta said and put the file folder into a drawer on the right side of her desk. "Just wanted to let you know that a decision has been made."

* *

Damon and Jeff didn't notice that no one had come into the break room during their discussion. People had finished eating and left – and they weren't replaced with new breakers. During the entire disease aversion discussion, they were the only two bodies in the room.

Damon and Jeff didn't notice the two men who entered the room right as the discussion ended.

Damon and Jeff didn't notice the third man standing at the door, making sure no one else came in.

The two men were dressed smartly. Well-creased gray slacks, light blue polo shirts, dark blue suitcoats.

"Damon Butcher," one man said, extending a hand. "My name's Marcus Osborne. I work for Allied Genetics. With your friend. Miles Lofton."

"Oh, sure," Damon said, looking crossways at Jeff, extending his own hand to shake Osborne's. "Is everything okay?"

"Sure. Sure. Fine," Marcus said. "I was hoping we could have a private conversation. Take five minutes of your time."

"Sir," the as-yet-unnamed man indicated that Jeff should leave with him.

Jeff looked at Damon as if to ask, *Should I stay?*

14

Damon shook his head as if to answer, *Nah*.

"I'm going to need to buy a soda in about five minutes," Jeff said, before turning to leave.

Marcus pulled out a chair for Damon and then sat down on the opposite side of the table. He waved his hand and smiled.

"Please," he said. "Really, nothing's wrong. I just need to talk to you for a moment."

* *

"You want to offer me a job?" Damon asked after Marcus gave his speech. "I have a job. In case you didn't notice. You probably should have called." Damon looked around. "I'm not even sure this is ethical, you offering me a job at my current work."

"It's okay," Marcus said. "My boss can be very convincing. I just need a moment of your time, as I said. Any deeper conversation can be concluded after your shift."

During the discussion, Marcus had taken a folded piece of paper out of his pocket and slid it across the table top. Damon noticed, but didn't take the paper. He also paused to look around the room briefly. It was bizarre to be alone in a room so big—a room that is never actually empty. Marcus, having said his peace, remained quiet. He had adopted a relaxed posture and rested the palms of his hands flat on the table. Damon noticed a small tattoo on the web of skin between the man's right thumb and right index finger. It was a crude image of a scorpion. Well-drawn, but poorly applied. Perhaps it was a prison tattoo. Or something soldiers would give each other in the field.

"I like my job," he continued, his voice echoing off the hard surfaces of the room—no bodies were there to diffuse the sound. "I'm loyal to Precision."

Marcus continued to smile and watched Damon, eye to eye.

Damon broke eye contact again and looked at the piece of paper. It looked like a computer printout, folded into thirds, ready to go into an envelope. The folds were crisp, but it was slightly open. Damon could see text printed on the face of the paper. He could just make out a piece of the letterhead before it was enveloped in shadow.

"I'm loyal…" he trailed off and squinted at the paper and completely shut one eye as if he was a pirate or a sniper glaring through a scope. It was an unconscious habit he had picked up years ago. It was first developed for comedic effect, but soon became a part of who he was.

He reached forward and held the paper between his thumb and index finger.

"It can't hurt just to read the actual offer," he said, unfolding the paper.

CHAPTER THREE
THE LAB

"BASED PURELY on volume, this facility is easily the largest man-made structure in Crimea," Miles said as the two men walked down a corridor.

The floors were polished concrete and the walls were pure industrial. They were a mixture of concrete, steel girders, copper piping, and various bundles of cabling running off into the distance. The corridor itself was wide enough for a military vehicle to pass easily with plenty of room on either side to spare.

Damon had visited numerous facilities in his short career, but this area easily outpaced them all.

"The Russians started building Objekt 221 at the height of their Cold War spending," Miles continued. "It was to be the home of the Soviet Army's Black Sea fleet. Straddling an area roughly translated as Anvil Canyon. Something about the materials that used to be mined here. The complicated network of tunnels and bunkers forced them to essentially hollow out huge sections of Mount Misen. It was a back-up command facility with two entrances and four levels. It was built to withstand even the most horrifying theoretical bomb the United States could drop on it. Unfortunately, it was never properly finished."

They continued walking down the main corridor. There were doors on either side of the space and bustling activity all around them. There was a mixture of directions, eagerness, and outfits. Some people in lab coats were hurrying to and fro, while others walked in a leisurely manner, chatting with co-workers. At odd intervals, Damon noticed people wearing what could only be described as military outfits. There were no symbols, flags, or insignia, but the material and gunbelts were unmistakable.

For their part, Miles and Damon looked like two peas in a pod. Dressed similarly in jeans and polo shirts, roughly the same height and weight. Both had brown hair and were in their early 30s. Miles wore glasses and had longer hair. They could be brothers.

Damon continued gazing around as Miles filled him in on the abbreviated history of the enormous facility.

"Construction was terminated in 1989—same year as the fall of the Berlin Wall—and was buttoned up. Battalions of workers were released back into the wild to fend for themselves. Jobless. It was estimated that the facility was 80 percent completed. Unlike her sister facility—Objekt 825—which was finished and eventually reimagined as a Naval Museum in Balaklava. There are abandoned facilities like this scattered all around the world." Miles paused and shot Damon a sideways glance. Damon didn't notice. "Many of them repurposed."

They continued to walk and the end of this particular corridor was finally in sight. Also, the tone of the hallway had subtly changed. Office and laboratory doors had disappeared from the left side to be replaced with a huge display case. The lighting, somehow, was also softer now. And a little darker.

It was an enormous terrarium.

Damon edged closer to the display case and slowed his pace, but didn't stop. There was some mist on the inside of the window and he could see that the case was set into the wall about two meters deep. Plants, forward and backward. The terrarium—two meters deep by nearly 20 meters long—was completely filled with flora. There was one problem, though, and Damon finally stopped to look.

"What the hell is this?" he asked. "I don't recognize any of these plants."

The case was filled with small trees, flowering plants, heavy bushes, and other generic greenery. It was beautiful in an unkempt way. As if someone had originally planned where to plant the flora, but then never landscaped the area again.

Miles smiled.

"Gorgeous, isn't it?" he asked, standing next to Damon, hands clasped behind his back.

Damon was looking back and forth, his nose mere inches from the glass.

"Seriously. I don't recognize any of these plants. Are they native here? From some previously undiscovered tropical island?"

Miles nodded.

"You have a good eye, man," he said. "These are from here but not *when.*"

Damon kept looking. He was now focused on one plant in particular. It had hand-sized leaves making up its base with two huge spires poking out the top. The base leaves were colored five or six different shades of green, and the spires were a tint of purple that he'd never seen before. He was examining the plant while Miles' words slowly sunk in.

"Not from *when*?" Damon asked and then thought for another moment. "When. These plants are extinct? You've somehow mutated them? Revived them somehow?"

Miles smiled.

"Yes and no. Not exactly," he said. "Let's keep walking."

* *

"You know the idiot part of Jurassic Park?"

Miles and Damon had walked past the terrarium of extinct flora and the corridor had fully returned to its normal state—regular lighting and doors on both sides of the hallway. Damon's mind was racing, quietly, behind his ever-watchful eyes. This was no longer a trip around the enormous facility—there was something now troubling about what was going on. He had just passed a huge display case filled to the brim with living examples of extinct plants. He wasn't sure what was coming next, and was only half-listening to Miles.

"What?" Damon asked. "The book or the movie? And which movie?"

"Either," Miles answered without missing a step. "Either story. Entire series. Same flaw."

Damon shrugged.

"I'm a bigger fan of Crichton than Spielberg."

Miles nodded.

"Storytellers, both, but they share the same affliction. They get too caught up with the dino DNA, right? Thousands of words in the book explain what's going on and scene after scene in the movie. There's one critical flaw in the story, though."

Miles paused as if he wanted Damon to come to the right conclusion. Damon, for his part, was keen to show his college buddy that his mind wasn't reeling from what he had just seen.

"The irrational frog-DNA leap?"

Miles shook his head.

"Nah. This wasn't even mentioned in the book. Or movie." He walked three more steps in silence. "I'll give you a hint. Assume that you could create the dinosaurs. What then?"

Damon thought for a moment.

"The environment."

Miles smiled and nodded.

"Yep. You got it. Sort of. I'll explain. In truth, the air would kill them." They continued walking toward the quick-approaching end of the hallway. "Assuming all of the other stuff was possible, the atmospheric composition was quite different a hundred million years ago. Not only the air composition, but the particulate matter—everything. All of those movies like Signs or War of the Worlds—remember the big reveal? How Earth is able to defeat the alien intruders? It's the Earth itself that kills the aliens."

Damon was smiling. He and Miles had had numerous conversations that went similarly at Berkeley. A study break. Relaxing over a Papi Blast pizza.

"Like oxygen. Almost a quarter of our atmosphere," he said. "A truly toxic gas that literally eats metal. We've evolved to breathe it, but it would absolutely *melt* a weary space traveler."

"Yeah." Miles laughed. "Exactly. Jurassic Park, or, more accurately, Cretaceous Park, pulls a mixture of dinosaurs and plants into the modern era...."

"The quaternary."

"Yes, of course. Into the quaternary era from the Mesozoic, before the K-Pg Extinction. The air likely contained much less oxygen and much higher levels of carbon dioxide. As well as elevated temperatures in general."

Damon glanced back at the terrarium.

"I thought the air during dinosaur times had a higher concentration of oxygen," he said. "I thought the theory was that the added oxygen was one of the reasons the big lizards grew so huge. Gigantism, I remember reading."

Miles shook his head.

"Not so. Current estimates put the oxygen concentration closer to 10 percent. Much lower than our current 21 percent."

They continued walking forward, now at the end of the corridor. There was one door at the head of the corridor that was secured via keypad, voiceprint, and handprint panel. On the right-hand wall was a panel that was roughly two-meter by two-meter square. There was a small panel to the right of the door labeled "Auxiliary 5B."

"The dinosaurs couldn't breathe," Damon said quietly, almost to himself.

With a huge grin on his face, Miles reached over and pressed the green button on the auxiliary control surface. The panel slid back.

"Yep," Miles said. "That's why we need to wear these when we go back."

As the square metal panel split down the middle and slid to the left and right into the surrounding walls, Damon just looked on with wide-open eyes. Miles' last comment—taken in conjunction with what the open panel revealed—was starting to sink in.

Behind the steel panel were 20 face masks lined up nicely on hooks. Shatter-proof acrylic. Hermetically sealed. Temperature resistant. Each mask had a notch in the bottom that held a canister roughly the size of a can of soda. The bottom of the opening was lined with nearly 100 such canisters. They were labeled O4BC – Breathable Air.

"Oh shit," Damon said.

"You're going to have fun working here." Miles smiled.

* *

"Christ on a cracker," Britta said, leaning forward in her desk chair.

She was sitting in the comfortable leather chair with Marcus Osborn and Jason Beale flanking her, slightly behind. They had each watched the video a dozen times, but this was the first time it had been presented to the boss.

Marcus was holding a tablet, inputting commands. The video image on Britta's laptop screen came to its conclusion and froze.

She didn't move, remaining pitched forward in her chair, only the balls of her feet resting on the floor.

"Run that back again," Britta said to Marcus without turning her head.

They had watched footage of Building 5's west corridor from this morning. It was mostly footage from Beale's visor camera, but also elements of the rest of his team's recordings.

The blood smears.

The destroyed gear.

The 10-foot predator.

Uncategorized.

Four heavily muscled arms.

Giant, spiked tail.

Eating a world-class soldier like an after-school snack.

The amalgamated footage ran its course a second time.

"Data is set to burst-upload," Marcus said, again, pressing commands on his tablet. "We're having trouble retrieving the visuals from Harrison's team."

Britta, again, not looking back at the two men, addressed them.

"You find me footage of the attack and you find out what was causing your glitch." She reached forward and wound the video back to an earlier portion. She froze the screen on a ghastly image—when the sensor had first picked up the predator. It was standing in the harsh light of the camera, chewing on the shoulder of a headless warrior. Blood and gore were dripping down its jaws, coating its chest.

Marcus gave a small shudder—it was a horrifying image. Beale just looked at him and shrugged.

"The egg-heads are running their version of the recordings through the necessary filters," Beale said. "Prelim results are in the folder. They're calling it UC-0104 until they can get a clear picture of what's going on."

Britta put her hand on the folder and slid it closer to her laptop. Finally, she turned to look back at the men.

"When are you going back out?" she asked Beale.

He shrugged.

"There's nothing on the schedule as yet, ma'am," he said. "NR-401G was the final specimen on the current order sheet. I'm sure they're working up a new list, but there's been nothing approved so far. It's SOP (standard operating procedure) to give the men 48 hours downtime between excursions."

Britta nodded.

"When do you think they'll be ready to grab one of these?" she said with a head-bob toward the monstrosity that dominated her laptop screen.

Beale shrugged.

"All due respect, no idea. It's been a while since the lab coats have come up against a predator of this nature. The last time, it took about two weeks—four missions—to gain enough data to try and snag one. Ma'am."

She nodded.

"Right. I remember. CX-2978. I'll talk to Carter later and see about coming up with a schedule." She looked from Marcus to Beale and back. "Thank you both for bringing me this data so quickly."

The two men nodded and took the hint that they were excused. After they had left the office and closed the door, Britta leaned forward, pushed the laptop about a foot further across the desk, and rested her elbows on the surface. She put her chin on her two balled-up fists and stared intently at the laptop screen.

"Well, fuck," she said.

And then smiled.

* *

The lab was bustling with activity and Miles didn't seem to notice. He led Damon across the huge room, past numerous partitions piled high with both chemical and electronic workstations, and to a corner desk. There were separate rooms walled off, but they seemed to Damon to be reserved for toxic or otherwise dangerous experiments. There were no private offices in the lab.

This, however, was clearly Miles' desk. Lofton sat in the rolling chair and waved Damon to one of the two plush red leather visitor's chairs. Damon sank about an inch into the rich padding.

"Okay," he said, looking across the desk at his college friend. "What the fuck?"

Miles smiled.

"Hah hah, yeah. Usually, the process is a little more, um, gentle. People are recruited for months or even years. Your recruitment, though, was about 45 minutes. We need you, man. We're on the brink of something big and we need your cross-section of talent."

"Blah, blah, blah," Damon said. "We're talking dinosaurs, time travel, and abandoned Russian military bases. Is there anything else I should know about? Sentient toasters? Android prostitutes?"

Miles, still smiling, shook his head.

"No, nothing so crazy. But you gotta admit—that's the bad-ass trifecta, though, right?" He paused for a moment, leaned forward, and rested his forearms on the desk. "Allied Genetics is on the forefront of a lot of advanced technology all across the world. This facility is the crown jewel of the company—where all of the latest research is funneled—but it remains only Alpha Complex. O221. Anvil Canyon."

"Okay, sure," Damon said. "How about we go to the next piece of the puzzle. You explained Objekt 221. Talk to me about traveling back in time."

Miles sighed.

"I've got a room with about 300 inches of binder space dedicated to nothing but equations that I can let you read through, but I'll spare you the exciting details." He smiled. He knew that one of the first things Damon would do was read through all of that data. "Thumbnail version for now?"

"Yeah," Damon said. "Sure. Get me in that neighborhood and then I can figure out the rest while unearthing my role here."

Miles nodded.

"Fair enough." He paused as if summoning the strength to give the same speech he'd given a dozen times before. "There are soft spots in the world. Places where electromagnetic energy is focused. Places where life and plasma and karma and energy and all that seem to come together causing strange connections."

"You're talking about ley lines. The Vile Vortices. The Bermuda Triangle. Stuff like that?"
"Sure. Yeah. You're on the right track. The natural, metaphysical properties of these places—when combined with modern and ultra-modern technology—can lead to extraordinary results. Objekt 221—perhaps unbeknownst to the original designers, perhaps they knew—sits atop one of the strongest phenomena in the northern hemisphere."

Damon remained silent. Rubbed his chin.

"We learned that with the right balance of heavy energy, we could travel through these soft spots, these rifts, into the past."

Miles stopped as if he was expecting Damon to ask a question. Damon had a question, but he wasn't sure if it was the one Miles was waiting for. He decided to ask it anyway.

"We might be getting to this," he said. "But if you can travel through time, why are you collecting plants rather than killing Hitler or preventing 9/11 or derailing the extinction of the spotted huckaloo? Seems there are millions of things you could be doing. Is it because of the grandfather paradox? The butterfly effect?"

"Hah," Miles exclaimed. "The butterfly effect. You're adorable."

"What?"

"There is no such thing, rookie. Think about it. What's the central tenet of the theory? A butterfly flaps its wings in Beijing and there's a rainstorm in Nebraska? Nope. It's a fun idea, but any big system—the stock market, weather, life—is going to absorb those types of small changes and proceed on its intended course. The fun is determining if it was going to rain in Nebraska whether the butterfly got stepped on or not."

"Cascading changes. Growing ripples. Every decision we make impacts those around us in ways we can't even imagine."

Miles was smiling and shaking his head.

"Save the planet," he said, and paused.

"What's that supposed to mean?"

"Look," Miles said, rubbing the palms of his hands together. "We're going to have a ton of these types of conversations, so I'll cut to the chase. You, as a human, would have to do something *enormous* to even have a small chance at causing a ripple effect. We're not talking about stepping on a butterfly—we're talking about stepping on *every* butterfly. We're not talking about breaking a branch—we're talking about burning down *every tree on the planet*. Something of that magnitude. So, no, your butterfly effect is just not real. The world simply absorbs those small changes and continues on its intended course."

"Hmm," Damon grunted. "Okay, leaving all that aside, since the Earth moves through time and space, how are you not reconstituted on another part of the planet—or, for that matter, hurtling through outer space in the past?"

"Now *that's* a great question," Miles said. "And the truth is that we don't know. Not exactly. It has something to do with the Earth's magnetic core keeping us grounded. In conjunction with the fact that the rift is somehow stable, we always come back to the same area on the planet. Roughly the same time."

"Hmm."

"And that gets to another point you made," Miles continued. "You asked why we don't go and kill Hitler or prevent the Kennedy assassination. Our rift sends us to the same era. Over and over again. The Cretaceous. That's just an element of the phenomenon. It's our designated research spot."

He paused for a second.

"We can discuss the nature of a true time paradox later."

Damon sat back in his chair. He looked around the small office area. Rather mundane desk. Average chairs. Miles was some sort of supervisor, but you couldn't really tell from his personal office space. There were a few framed internal letters. A couple awards. Some items with the Cal logo on them. There was a signed football with UC Berkeley branding on it resting on the top of an over-stuffed bookcase near the wall. No family photos.

Damon leaned forward, a question suddenly becoming apparent.

"What's the goal, here?" he asked.

Miles held out his hands, fingers splayed wide, palms toward Damon.

"Strictly observational. We collect data and continue to build a coherent picture of the Cretaceous period. Eventually, we'll release our findings to the world for educational purposes."

Damon sat back.

"Okay," he said. "Great." Even though he knew, instinctively, that wasn't true. Whether Miles was intentionally lying or he simply hadn't put two-and-two together, Damon knew there was more at stake than simple observation. An uncanny valley of information had just formed.

CHAPTER FOUR
THE MYSTERIOUS ISLAND

PORT RADNOVICH was a postage stamp floating unfettered amidst the enormity of the Gulf of Mexico. It was 150 kilometers southwest of the extreme tip of Florida and was too small to show up on all but the most efficient satellite searches. Even so, the government quietly scrubbed the tiny island from all surveys and published maps in 1975.

The island essentially covered the same surface area as the city of Los Angeles and was, for all intents and purposes, uninhabited. However, even with the questionable significance, dubious importance and nonexistent strategic positioning, Port Radnovich was about to be invaded.

In the dead of night, the Wraiths came. It was a massacre.

* *

Sergott Solutions was a multinational conglomerate—a worldwide security force. With hundreds of ex-military and ex-law enforcement officers on the payroll, SS stood ready to provide security for events from mundane birthday parties held in dangerous neighborhoods to political debates in regional hotspots. If you had the money, Sergott had a solution for you.

As profitable as protection was to this organization, they also maintained a highly trained para-military force known internally as the Wraiths. With the best weaponry, most expensive gear, and intense training regimen, the Wraiths were often hired out for the jobs that couldn't look like a job.

Made up of a strange combination of Navy SEALs, British SAS, Russian Alpha Group, and Israeli Mossad, the Wraiths were rumored to have been involved in dozens of military coups, hostage liberations, and terrorist cell eliminations.

Rumored, but never proven.

Now, an assault force of six Wraiths was sent in advance of a 25-man support team in the occupation of Port Radnovich.

* *

The island was no bigger than a large American city but had four interesting features. One, a clearly marked—yet horribly overgrown and positioned in the worst strategic part of the island—concrete helicopter landing pad. Two, a long, straight path of prairie grasses that looked totally unremarkable, unless, of course, you happened to be approaching the island in a small, single-engine aircraft. Three, the ruins of a large dock on the only protected side of the island. Four, a single-story building with no windows, one door, and walls made of a meter-thick combination of steel and concrete.

Curiously, an armed sentry stood guard outside this solitary door.

Wraith Field Commander Rick "Ahab" Everson held his force back from the door. They took cover and his recon man started using whatever equipment—night vision, thermal vision, field glasses—was available to assess the situation. In 30 minutes, Lonny "Doc" Watley came back to the team.

"Intelligence was accurate, sir," Doc said, quietly, into his throat microphone. "He's armed with an MP-5. Holstered Colt. Wearing NVG."

Ahab Everson nodded. He looked down at his watch and then up to the sky.

"Full dark," he said. "Shift change in 20. Get in position."

The other five men nodded and split up into their pre-arranged spots.

* *

Nineteen and a half minutes later, the door opened and the second sentry emerged from the low concrete building. It was not SOP, but he left the thick steel door open behind him. The two men were backlit as they talked but, more importantly, it rendered their night vision nearly useless. The man going off shift bummed a cigarette and they both stood and laughed—recounting stories of the day.

"Now," Ahab whispered into his throat mic.

Pop, pop.

Kill, kill.

The two sentries dropped to the ground and the six Wraiths immediately moved in. The two men were dragged around the corner of the building and covered with a thermal blanket printed with jungle camouflage. When the dead men were stored away, all six soldiers stacked up alongside the door of the building. Willie Cole, call sign Salad, brought up a small wrist-mounted computer and started tapping away.

"Connection established," Salad said. He was looking at the LCD screen on the unit, rapidly pressing different commands. "Cameras are down."

Immediately after he said that, all six Wraiths entered the small concrete building.

Even though they had read the intelligence reports, they were awe-struck.

* *

It was a missile silo. Built in 1972. Designed to lay waste to Cuba. Abandoned in 1987. Purchased by Allied Genetics in 2009. According to internal reports, the facility was referred to as "Frenchman's Flat."

The Wraiths were hired to murder everyone in the facility and capture any research that was being done.

"Countdown begins," Salad said quietly. "Twelve minutes." He sat down at the main security terminal in the corner of the room. At this time of night, Frenchman's Flat was unmanned and security was performed by a combination of the sentries and automated systems.

He immediately started tapping away at the keyboard in front of him, quietly and quickly unraveling various security features, allowing his team access to the entire facility.

The heavy steel door slid shut with a muffled *whump*.

Ahab Everson checked his wrist computer, as did the rest of his team. There was a line of 20 faces with red Xs over the two sentries killed at the front door. Eighteen more to go.

He looked over the aluminum railing and then back to the rest of his team.

"Alright," he said. "Time to make dreams come true."

* *

The squat building in the center of Port Radnovich was little more than a stair-head. The interior was spacious, but the single room was dominated by a hole in the middle of the floor, ringed by a circular staircase that ran loops 12 stories deep. There was one door, a security cubicle, and a freight elevator—which Salad had shut down after verifying it was empty.

Commander Everson led the four other team members quickly and quietly down the stairs. Personal preferences aside, the Wraiths were equipped identically for this mission. They each wore Sig MPX SBR submachine guns across their chests and Sig M25 Navy handguns in thigh holsters. The other thigh was reserved for a combat knife with a proven military history popularized by the Marines—the Ka-Bar. Half of the men crept down the stairs holding their knives, the other half held the handguns. Cole would regularly call out system updates from his position on the top floor.

The Wraiths only needed to worry about three floors, numbered in elevator opposite. The lowest floor of the facility, floor 12, was the server farm with two tech employees who were at this very moment, under siege from Salad Cole. Floor 8, at this time of the night, should be home to three researchers. Floor 2, the floor right beneath them, was residential. The rest of the researchers and four additional sentries would be on this floor. Hopefully, soundly asleep.

The six men split up. Salad stayed on 1. One man took up station at the entrance of the residential quarters on 2. One man hid outside the research facility on 8. The remaining three Wraiths went all the way down to the server room on 12. The men on 1, 2, and 8 would simply stay on sentry as the killing started on the bottom floor and moved up. Anyone trying to escape would be taken down by Salad as they ran for the exit door.

"Floor 12. Mark," Ahab spoke softly into his throat mic.

"All clear, sir," came the response from Salad more than 100 feet— 30 meters—above him.

The commander nodded to the two soldiers who had taken up position outside of the server room. They slid a UV camera under the door and the image immediately popped up on their wrist computers.

The three men looked at each other and shared a nod. A silent signal for, *good to go*.

* *

The server room was shockingly cold. And loud. The Wraiths had noticed the temperature change as they traveled deeper and deeper into the bowels of the facility's singular vertical structure—possibly the reason why the residential quarters were near the top. The server room, however, was even colder than it should be. Just by looking at the three silent, black-clad soldiers, though, you'd be hard-pressed to see their discomfort.

There were two men sitting on the north end of the server room. They were both hammering away at their respective keyboards, clearly frustrated by something. They were yelling at each other. They were likely encountering whatever problem Cole had cooked up for them from his access to the system. Additionally, they had to shout over the hum of the powerful HVAC units that cooled the massive computer towers. They were completely distracted and had no idea that the enemy soldiers had entered the room.

Two of the Wraiths took position. They were under orders not to damage any of the equipment, so firepower was to be kept to a minimum in the server room as well as the research facility. They had each taken Ka-Bars in their right hands. In a practiced, synchronized move, the two soldiers slit the throats of the two server-men. They died in seconds, slumped forward in their chairs.

Silent.

Fatal.

* *

Ahab and his two soldiers left the server room and traveled up the circular staircase to Floor 8 – Research. The three men met up with the soldier already in position outside the door of the lab. The man, James "Smooth Money" Racine looked back at Ahab and spoke softly.

"Three men," he said. "Two working together on the north end. One solo, southwest corner. No other movement."

The commander nodded and touched his earpiece.

"Overwatch."

"Clear on 8, sir," Salad spoke, staring intently at his surveillance monitors. "Intel is good."

Ahab Everson nodded again. He pointed at his two men from the server room mission and pointed toward the north end of the research area. He pointed to Smooth Money and indicated that he would take out the solitary man in the southwest. The three men nodded in unison.

On the main floor, Salad pulled up his list of 20 workers—down to 18—and touched the images of the two men who lay slain in the bowels of Frenchman's Flat. Two more red Xs. Sixteen workers.

* *

Compared to the server room, the research lab was a library. The soldiers could hear various computer fans kicking on and off and the random clink of metal on metal or glass on glass, but the ambient noise was virtually nonexistent. It was the same with discussion. Whereas the two server workers had been screaming at each other while fighting to resolve their computer problems, the three researchers went about their business in silence.

Now, inside the large space, all Wraith verbal communication was halted. They, all three, knew their assignments. Rick "Ahab" Everson stayed back a few yards in from the door, totally concealed, as a failsafe: No one was coming in and no one was getting out.

The three soldiers—Smooth Money, Twelve, and Bounce—silently made their way through the research lab, knives in hand. Just like the server room, they were under strict orders to not damage anything. The support team would be coming in as soon as the facility was clear of enemy personnel to take care of hard evidence. Little things, however, kept catching their attention. Even though they maintained strict focus on the task at hand, it was hard to ignore:

Five giant glass bottles filled with liquids of various colors—the fifth liquid was bubbling with no apparent heat source.

A dissected octopus, under glass, that turned out to be robotic.

Several colorful posters warning about the spread of CX disease.

Three laptops, linked together with heavy cables, which seemed to be running a virus outbreak simulation. A small line of masking tape ran along the top of one monitor. "The Event: Pandemic" was written on it in black ink.

One large metal container that occupied a corner of the room. It was covered with caution symbols, radiation symbols, and skulls. It also had what appeared to be breathing holes cut into the top three inches. A strange machine sat to the side of the huge metal box, humming with power. Thick cables ran from the machine to the base of the container.

Nevertheless, the team advanced on the three researchers.

Twelve and Bounce rushed the two men who were working together, knives raised, in the same practiced synchronicity displayed in the server room. Smooth Money was creeping up behind the lone man—he was five feet away. With the three soldiers in position, Ahab called out the kill order—a whisper picked up by their high-definition throat mic.

It looked like something out of a training manual. Throats slit from behind, left to right, at exactly the same moment. All three researchers went down in a heap. The three Wraiths wiped the blood off their knives on the dead men's clothing as their commander entered the center of the room.

He surveyed the same strange objects that his men had seen.

Suddenly, there was a thump from inside the large metal cage.

The three soldiers immediately raised their SMGs. Ahab raised his hand.

"Leave it," he said quietly into his throat mic. "Salad. What do we have on a possible biological under lock and key in the research lab?"

"Looking, sir," came the reply from their overwatch position. He was furiously tapping away at one computer while keeping an eye on the final stage of the mission on another. "Multiple references to Specimen NR-401G, but specific data is encrypted. I can get to it, if you'd like, sir."

"Negative, soldier. We leave it for support to deal with."

"Understood, sir."

* *

With Salad still on the main floor, the five remaining black-clad insurgents grouped outside the sleeping quarters on the second floor. They knew there were nine sleeping workers and two sleeping security personnel. There were two sentries that were awake playing cards at a small table near the front of the room, illuminated by a small desk lamp.

With the firefight restrictions removed for this final room, the five Wraiths held their Sig submachine guns at the ready. They were stacked up outside the main entrance—three on one side, two on the other. They waited for the all-clear signal from their overwatch, and when it came, they stormed the room.

It was, as expected, a massacre.

The two woke guards were the first to go down, followed by the two sleeping guards. After that, the five Wraiths moved through the sleeping quarters eliminating the nine scientists. After the first shots were fired, it quickly became chaos. With the main door locked, Salad crouched behind his security console with his weapon at the ready. He watched both the security monitors and the physical stair-head. No one was getting out of Frenchman's Flat alive.

The acrid smells of gunpowder and blood filled the enormous room as the five-man advance team stalked the sleeping quarters. They were taking a final look to ensure nothing had been missed. Two of the men grabbed souvenirs—one was a small, metal Hot Wheels car, the other was a stuffed animal, a pig that rested on a bedside table. The team left as a group, stepping over the dead bodies that littered the floor.

* *

"Tree House, this is Firefly, come in."

Rick "Ahab" Everson had collected his team and all six Wraiths were huddled around the command console on the top floor of the facility. Per protocol, he was calling in his support team as a signal that the area was clear and prepped for stage two.

"This is Tree House. Go ahead, Firefly," came the response over the secure channel.

"Backyard is empty. Needs to be cleaned, over."

Salad and Twelve looked at each other and rolled their eyes. You never got used to goofy mission lingo.

"Copy that, Firefly. Tree House out."

Ahab turned to his team.

"Alright, men," he said, absently checking his combat gear to make sure everything was secured. "That just leaves the easy part. Wraiths, mount up."

And, with that, the advance team exited the building and jogged to their waiting extraction point...never to cross paths with the support team.

CHAPTER FIVE
THE WAYBACK MACHINE

"QUANTUM SPIRES?" Damon Butcher was carefully examining a digital computer readout on one monitor while feverishly manipulating the touchscreen of another computer monitor only a foot to his right.

"An inverted quantum spire, actually," Miles Lofton replied. "Basically a modified Sheffield Vortex." He paused to look at the readout that had caught Butcher's eye. "At least that's where the algorithm started. With Sheffield. We had to make certain adjustments. But it gave us a great head start."

"Wow." Butcher leaned back and exhaled deeply. "You guys did some amazing work in what looks like a relatively short amount of time."

Miles looked proud. His team couldn't take all the credit for the success of Allied Genetics, but they played a significant role.

Seemingly, for the first time, Damon looked around the room. Miles noticed this and started his speech where he had originally deviated.

"Before you suffered a cataclysmic attention opportunity, I was explaining about the launching pad," Miles said. Damon stood up and looked around the room, very possibly seeing it for the first time.

It was a large room, nearly a 15-meter square footprint. It sloped downward, away from the huge glass doors. There were 18 computer workstations angled in semi-concentric circles pointing toward the bottom of the room. The far wall was lined with huge monitors. They were nearly all inert, save for the top right which displayed the current day/time and the top left which displayed the current weather with four columns of detail. Damon noted, absently, that both screens were split in half, diagonally, and seemed to show vastly different numbers.

The floor in front of the monitors—nearly a quarter of the square footage of the room—was striking. The floor tiling was completed in stainless steel. It was an octagonal shape and each side was punctuated by a two-meter-tall antenna. This area was known as the launching pad and could very nearly fill the space of a typical residential bedroom.

"Graviton dissonance," Miles Lofton said.

"Huh? What's that?" Damon said, turning to look at his former classmate. He had been staring at the launching pad, mentally analyzing every element in great detail.

"That bigger pillar over there," Miles said, indicating the pillar with a lift of his chin. "It generates a graviton dissonance that acts as our anchor to the Earth's magnetic core." He paused for effect. "You had brought it up earlier. How do we make sure that when we appear 100 million years in the past, we don't go flying off into space? Graviton dissonance."

Damon was nodding as Miles was speaking. In truth, his attention was fractured. He thought they had been on the cutting edge at Precision Robotics. This, however, was tech he had never dreamed of.

The room was buzzing with energy. Workers were filtering in through the giant glass doors at the head of the area and the huge monitors were coming to life. Miles put a hand on his friend's shoulder.

"Usually there's a ramp-up process," Miles said. "A transition period. But, I think you'd rather run before you can walk. We have an excursion planned in about four hours. How would you like to join us?"

The only answer Damon had evaporated as his mouth hung agape.

"I'll take that as a *yes*." Lofton smiled.

* *

It's been a long day, Miles had said, steering Damon back toward the door of the staging area. *This gentleman will show you to your room. Be back here in four hours.*

There was an entire floor of an entire wing devoted to residential needs. A couple cafeterias. A couple shops. Several laundromats. And enough rooms to dwarf a large apartment complex. Damon's room was actually four rooms. It was similar to a suite at a mid-level American hotel. Bedroom. Sitting room. Kitchenette. Plus a bathroom.

Damon unpacked his clothes, sprawled out on his bed, and tried to relax.

In a completely different wing, on a completely different floor, Britta Vragi was on the phone. She was watching the security footage from the unidentified predator on her computer with the sound off.

"Yeah," she said. "In four hours. The research team."

She was silent for a moment then nodded her head as if the person on the other end of the line could actually see her.

"Right. Strictly observational. They have no specific checklist." She paused, listening to the person on the other end. "Absolutely. And, Carter, Miles just informed me that they'll be taking the new guy with them."

She clicked the small icon on the bottom of her video player that started the action over at the beginning.

"Exactly. Let's get alpha team spun up first thing in the morning. I want another crack at this unknown."

She hung up her handset and leaned forward.

"Unreal," she said to the office, watching the massacre unfold before her.

* *

The four hours passed poorly for Damon Butcher. He took a nap. Fitfully. Tossing and turning. He turned on the streaming TV service. He read a magazine. He read a binder of dense calculations. Finally, he took a shower and got dressed in a fresh outfit.

And promptly got lost trying to find the staging area.

* *

The facemask was a shield—both in the physical resemblance to the shape and in the function of the piece itself. Damon admired it briefly before snapping it into place. There was a military-grade foam rubber seal that went around the wearer's face. The mask itself was held in place both by calculated negative pressure and thick Velcro straps— three of them—that met in the back of the head. The air canister held 12 hours of breathable air.

Once on and activated, the shatter-proof acrylic mask was overlaid with a pale yellow HUD that contained helpful information about the wearer's health, the surroundings, and the rest of the team. The mask contained both a microphone and speakers and a camera that ran continuously and burst-transmitted to the main server for storage every 12 minutes.

Everyone on the mission team was synched up through the control center and could speak to each other freely over an open channel. A single word command and password would open a secure channel to a selected team member.

If Allied Genetics ever ran low on cash reserves, they could sell these facemasks and make a billion dollars. Several times over.

Damon was suited up and snapped his facemask into place. He activated the oxygen canister and felt the mask suck in close to his face—a product of the negative pressure. He ran his hands down the rest of his uniform, although it was fairly mundane when compared to the futuristic facemask.

To outward appearances, he wore a camouflaged tactical suit with heavy black boots. A careful observer, however, would notice that there was absolutely no exposed skin. Thick boots that came to mid-shin. Heavy gloves. And a balaclava that went up behind the head and disappeared beneath the thick protective acrylic of the facemask. He wore a backpack stuffed full of helpful equipment.

There were five other members of the expedition team, all standing on the launching pad. All of the monitors against the far wall were up and running. The center console was counting down. Damon hadn't stopped smiling in the last four hours.

10.

9.

8.

"Here we go, man," Lofton said to Damon and, of course, the entire mission team. "This might feel a little weird the first time you go through it."

3.

2.

1.

White.

"Oh shit," Damon said, and didn't say, at the same time.

* *

He made it a point to stand perfectly still. Miles had told him to close his eyes before, during, and after the transition. He hadn't told him about the ringing in his ears—the way his entire head seemed to be vibrating. The way every hair on his body seemed to be standing on end. He had started counting when he heard the end of the countdown on the launching pad in Objekt 221.

"Warble baffle goop," came a voice over Damon's facemask speaker system. He shook his head, eyes still closed. "Baffle goop, ay-men."

He wanted to stick his fingers in his ears and try to pop the odd pressure he was feeling. Butcher had counted to 30 and was noticing that his senses were starting to return to normal.

"Ay-man, comepin," the voice was more insistent.

He was starting to hear words, though, and decided to reply.

"Miles?" he asked the team. "Mission team. This is Damon Butcher."

There was a popping sensation at the base of his neck and the general tingling feeling seemed to evaporate.

"Hope-in urice."

On a hunch, Damon slowly opened his eyes and took in his surroundings. His world snapped into place.

"Oh my God," he said.

"Yeah," Miles said, now standing right next to him. "Welcome to O221, Cretaceous version."

Damon was standing in the same position he had been on the launching pad. In truth, he was still on the launching pad. At some point, he had clenched his fists. Instead of staring at a wall of television screens, he was staring at a beautiful open vista through reinforced glass.

"Oh my God," he said again.

"Yeah," Miles said again and paused. "We don't know how it smells," he said thoughtfully. "We think it will smell similar to our world what with the flora, fauna, wild dinosaur poop, rot, biological decay—that sort of thing. But we're not sure. The plate does too good a job filtering all that stuff out."

"Plate?"

Miles tapped the side of his facemask.

"The mask. The faceplate," he said. "Just a nickname."

Damon nodded but never took his eyes off the wilderness surrounding him. It looked nothing like the Crimea that he had stood in two minutes ago.

He could tell almost instinctively that it was warmer. There was a glow about the plants—they glistened in the strong sunlight. And the sunlight. It was dazzling. Yet, somehow different.

"Higher concentration of both carbon dioxide and water in the atmosphere," Miles said. "We also seem to be in the midst of an oxygenation peak. The oxygen levels are toxic for humans right now. But the plants seem to be doing great."

Damon continued to scan the area. Trees, plants, bushes, flowers— some he even thought he recognized. The very beginnings of lush plains grasses. There seemed to be a mist covering much of the greenery. The sky had a strange orange-ish hue. He was shaken to his core when a dinosaur thundered across his field of vision—emerging from behind a thick group of trees on his left, lumbering across the 100-meter wide field, and disappearing into another grove on the right.

"Ahhh," Damon exhaled. On the HUD of his plate, a frozen image of the dinosaur, deteriorated into a wireframe, back to a full image. It reduced in size and text filled the screen.

AK1503.

Herbivore.

40-feet long.

28-feet tall.

Weight (est) 4.5 tons.

"I, uh," Damon said, both reading his screen and watching the live surroundings.

"Yeah," Miles said, chuckling. "It's. I know. It's a bit shocking to see them. We're used to seeing bones in a museum or, failing that, a best-guess recreation in a movie or video game. It's a bit different to see them take a dump right in front of you."

Damon was absently nodding.

"It looked like a *Spinosaurus*," Damon said. "But there was no name."

"Yep," Calvin, another researcher said who had walked up to join the two on the edge of the launching pad said. He was average height, thick build, dark hair. He was one of the senior men on the team. "It's a previously undiscovered species. Seems to be a distant relative of the *Spinosaurus*, or its herbivore cousin—*Ouranosaurus*. In the present day, they only have built a fossil record in Africa, but the time period is correct."

The dinosaur had been huge—similar to an elongated *Tyrannosaurus rex*. It had a long neck, long tail, and, across its back, was a razor-sharp sail of bone and leathery skin. Modern-day paleontologists were unsure whether this fin was used to attract mates, to aid in body temperature regulation, or a completely different purpose. Damon had a feeling that he would soon learn the reason for the spiny sail.

Most shocking, though, had been the coloring.

"The colors," Damon said, playing with the settings on the side of his plate and trying to rewind the recorded footage.

AK1503 was gorgeous.

Rather than the drab green coloring typified by modern lizards, this creature was beautiful and shared many of the characteristics of a snake. It had a pattern of green, white, brown, and orange shapes all along its skin and down its tail.

"We're only here for observation," Calvin continued after a moment. "In case you were wondering why it's called AK1503 rather than some creative nomenclature. Observe, codify, document."

Miles nodded in response.

"Exactly," he said, and then looked around the room, trying to see it as a new employee would. "So, this is pretty much a replica of the O221 staging area and control room. On this side of the equation, however, most of the computer stations are unmanned, and you can see that the wall monitors have been replaced by ultra-strength shatter-proof glass."

Damon was looking around the room, slowly coming out of his haze.

"Yeah, right."

"Plus, this facility is only a fraction of the size of our home base at Anvil Canyon. It's this room. A couple residential quarters. What we call a 'quicklab.' And a general maintenance room."

Damon turned toward a sign above three computer stations that read "Drone Control."

"Drones?" he asked the team.

Calvin nodded.

"Dangerous weather. Mating rituals. Feeding frenzies," he said. "Sometimes it makes more sense to film remotely than go out into the wild."

There was silence for a few moments.

"Okay." Miles smiled. "Enough foreplay. Let's get outside."

* *

On the right side of the room, on the immediate edge of the enormous viewing window, was an oversized door. Nearly six feet across and eight feet tall, it looked industrial…and totally out of place in this modern-tech environment. Heavy steel, visible pneumatic hinges, thick rubber piping to ensure an airtight seal—this door led to the airlock that led to the outdoors.

The four researchers were milling about near the door, waiting for their mission commander—Miles Lofton—and the new recruit—Damon Butcher—to get in line and officially begin the excursion. There were two men—Calvin Brunarski, Lazlo Hollyfeld—and two women—Cadey Park, Emi Tolliver. They were all four brilliant in their fields and had 10 advanced degrees between them.

"Okay," Miles said, signing some documentation and placing a clipboard on a nearby workstation. "It's go time."

CHAPTER SIX
THE OTHER TEAM

WITHOUT ALL the bells and whistles, the floorplan of Objekt 221 resembled a giant capital letter K. Originally, the straight, vertical spine of the letter would have represented two separate entrances—one at each of the extreme points of the facility. The northern entrance was recently closed off with four meters of reinforced concrete. Now there was one entrance and three spikes labeled Alpha, Beta, and R&D. The workers in these three areas weren't forbidden to talk to each other, but everyone was cautioned to not discuss the more sensitive elements of their work.

Britta's office was at the intersection of the four line segments, on the second floor. Right now, she was meeting with three other department heads and trusted colleagues. Marcus Osborne was her head of personnel. Carter Wittington was her operations manager. Jason Beale was the head of Alpha Team—the military branch of Objekt 221—made up almost exclusively of retired Army Rangers. They were, all four, sitting around a small meeting table that dominated the side of her office opposite the massive desk.

"So, NR-405G will be the final specimen on the next list," Carter said, making a checkmark on a legal pad and then flipping closed the leather portfolio he had been making notes on. On the cover was the stylized AG logo of Allied Genetics. He clipped his pen to the outside spine of the book.

"Got it," Marcus said, likewise making a checkmark on his list. Open in front of him was a thick Franklin Covey planner, leather-bound and loaded with notes. "I have it starting on Wednesday." He checked his watch. "Almost exactly 70 hours from now. Your team will be ready?"

He looked at Beale who simply nodded. Unlike the other two men, he had squared off a beaten-up steno pad and a ballpoint pen that was missing its cap. The steno pad had certainly seen better days with notes covering each page, coffee stains dotting the notes, and half-torn pages turned this way and that.

"Yeah," Beale said. "We're good with that timeframe. Standard deployment?"

It was Carter's turn to nod.

"Standard 10," he said.

"Good," Beale said. Like Carter, Marcus had closed his planner. Britta had no notes in front of her.

Everyone stood to leave and Britta finally broke her silence. She had offered no input during this short planning session, but wanted to discuss something before everyone adjourned for the day.

"We need to…" she said, and paused while the three men sat back down and got situated in their seats. "We need to discuss UC-0104," she continued.

"That thing that ate three of my men?" Beale asked.

"Yes," she replied. "I think we should bring one in."

There was silence around the short conference table. Her authority was unquestioned, and that was partly because she never gave unreasonable orders.

"What?" Marcus was the first to hazard a response.

Britta smiled and nodded in response, not to just Marcus but to the other two men as well.

"I know, I know, hear me out," she said. "An uncategorized apex predator with unmatched instincts and ferocity. Took down two highly trained, well-equipped soldiers without breaking a sweat. I think we need to study it. Could represent a huge leap forward in our research."

"It could also represent a huge leap forward in our mortality rate," Beale said.

"What about tagging one?" Marcus said, turning back a few pages in his planner. "R&D has developed a new version of Project Crimson. They're dying to test it out."

Britta leaned back in her chair, thinking.

"Okay," she said, nodding. "I'll compromise for now. Let's tag it." She looked directly at Carter. "I need you to examine every frame of that footage and start working on a containment strategy. We're going to eventually bring one of those in, and I want to be ready."

"Understood," Carter said.

CHAPTER SEVEN
THE HIDDEN TOWER

THAT THE German army constructed huge concrete towers in numerous locations around Europe was not a secret. It was hard to hide a 15-story structure with five-meter-thick walls. The secret part was that they had built four flak towers without anyone noticing.

There were a dozen towers that were well-known across several nations—some were even being repurposed all or in part. The four, though, that were built and never in operation, mostly stood rock-solid in their original locations. Three were in various forests on very secluded, enormous private properties. The fourth rested lazily at the bottom of a waterfall. While all the Nazi flak towers were special—historically, emotionally, and architecturally—the fourth tower, known as Hochhaus, or Sky Tower, was unique.

The construction of Hochhaus was finished just as the war ended. It was never operational. It was pristine. It was purchased by Allied Genetics in 1989.

It was now a research facility that was well-staffed, well-funded, and doing cutting-edge genetic modification experiments. Hybrid modifications. Human modifications. Illegal modifications.

Right now, the Wraiths were abseiling down the face of the waterfall. A stationary figure stood atop the waterfall "painting" the roof of the building with a green target. Six figures dressed all in black military clothing with advanced weaponry and futuristic tech rushed down the height of the waterfall silent and invisible.

Flak Tower Hochhaus was under attack—and it didn't even know it.

* *

Commander Alex "Beef" Scott lightly touched his throat mic.

"Team Big. Touchdown in 5, 4, 3…" He let the cadence continue silently. Beef reached the reinforced concrete rooftop of Hochhaus, followed by the silent landing of five more men. "Touchdown."

The seventh man, who would only be referred to as Overwatch during this mission, powered down his hand-held unit and the green targeting laser clicked off. He packed the small unit away in the combat webbing across the front of his gear and immediately pulled a small laptop out of his black canvas bag. He flipped it open, attached some power-boosted antennas to it, and turned it on.

Overwatch pulled one more item out of the bag and tossed it into the air. It powered up immediately and continued flying straight up into the air. It was a drone, barely larger than a man's shoe, with a camera and a strong broadcast signal.

Once the drone reached its broadcast height, the laptop screen flickered. It was a technical enhancement—a sensor that operated in night vision and thermal vision simultaneously.

Overwatch cracked his knuckles and reported in.

"Team Big," he said under his breath. "The bird is active."

"Understood, Overwatch," he heard the commander's voice in the tiny earpiece.

* *

Hochhaus was typical of the original flak tower commissions. It was 54 meters tall— taller than the Statue of Liberty—and had walls of reinforced concrete a fairly uniform 3.5 meters thick around the perimeter. The tower was designed to act as an air raid shelter for up to 10,000 people and had an operational defense range of 14 kilometers. Standing at the base of a waterfall, the structure was defended by a semi-circle of anti-tank measures. Where monstrous anti-aircraft guns had once stood atop the roof was a solid sheet of steel interrupted only by rebar-enforced termination grates of the air ventilation system.

Commanded by Alex "Beef" Scott, the six-man Wraith assault force prepared to infiltrate the facility they now stood atop.

Their orders were clear: No survivors.

Once the seven-man advance team cleared the facility, a clean-up team would sanitize the building and remove all relevant information. Commander Scott's involvement in the evening should last no longer than eight minutes.

* *

The design of the building, while innovative, was mostly borne out of the need for secrecy and protection. If it was a 15-story building, then the top three and bottom two floors stood empty.

These empty floors were masterfully disguised to look like an ongoing construction and renovation project…but were home to numerous defensive measures including EMP charges, auto-sentries, and strange little robots that looked like self-propelled vacuum cleaners with butcher knives attached to them.

All this, plus a host of guards. The Wraiths had received intel that 20 people would be in the building this evening. Much like the Port Radnovich facility. They had a similar plan, only compressed. They had a smaller footprint to deal with. Overwatch had a remote look at the facility through the uplink one of the members, Mack "Truck" Miller, had provided on the roof of Hochhaus. The rest of the team had prepared their ingress and waited for the signal.

"Commander, this is Overwatch."

"Go," replied Beef Scott into his throat mic.

"Intel confirmed. Twenty active keycards in the building. Sending you the schematic now."

Commander Scott looked down at his wrist display and it came to life as the new information was uploaded.

"Confirmed," the commander said.

It was four o'clock in the morning, roughly 24 hours since the assault on the repurposed missile silo at Port Radnovich. The facility known as Frenchman's Flat.

"Wraiths, we are a go."

* *

Overwatch remained at the top of the waterfall monitoring both electronics and the visual area via autonomous drone. The remaining six members of the Wraith squad had infiltrated the lowest floor of the flak tower. Their plan was to move floor to floor silently, killing everyone in their path. Another two dozen men would show up after the facility was clear. Their job was clean-up and extraction.

The plan, nearly immediately, went up in smoke.

"Oh shit," said Overwatch and Commander Scott simultaneously.

"Everybody down," Beef called to his team. Instinctively, all six men dove for cover in scattered directions.

Scott had seen in person what Overwatch had seen on his surveillance camera feed at the same time—the glint of ambient lighting hitting both the acrylic face-shield of a riot mask and the barrel of a

Metal Storm AICW assault rifle seconds before the room erupted in gunfire.

The AICW—Advanced Individual Combat Weapon—was developed by the Australian company, Metal Storm. It was the latest refinement in stacked munition technology. Each bullet was lined up end-to-end in the barrel and the weapon was capable of firing at an incredible rate.

As the Wraith team scattered for cover, Overwatch immediately keyed his mic—a direct link to the trailing support force.

"Commander Bilkins, we need you here now," he said. "Our team has encountered heavy opposition. An ambush."

"Copy that," Overwatch heard over the radio and then, "Move out, double-quick," before the support commander keyed off communications.

When the first facility had been attacked, a defensive contingency plan was implemented. Structural strategies were employed—designed to swing the advantage and thwart an offensive force. Namely, there were four men lying in wait behind heavy fortifications brandishing the latest in prototype weaponry.

Five of the six Wraiths made it to safety. The sixth man, Tim "Boss" Johnson, absorbed half a load of AICW bullets in an instant. Even with his body armor, Boss's torso was ripped to shreds by the high-velocity rounds.

Overwatch had immediately jammed Hochhaus' signals—inbound and outbound. There would be no calls for help. He wanted to jump into the battle and fight alongside his team, but the mission parameters clearly stated that he must remain in position.

The support force was five minutes out.

"Inbound," Overwatch said into his mission mic. "Team Juke. Four minutes, thirty-three."

"Copy that," Beef said. "Cross, Truck, start working your way to the right. The rest of you stay with me."

Ben "Cross" Christianson and Mack "Truck" Miller worked quickly to the right, avoiding enemy fire. Beef, Evan "Lugnuts" Hapwell and Wilson "Dandy" Reid provided cover fire. They fired sporadically as they were instinctively concerned about outlasting an entrenched enemy force.

The four Hochhaus men rotated to counter the natural flanking maneuver. Two fired in short bursts while the other two reloaded by changing the entire barrel of the AICW. Sparks flew around the room and chunks of concrete littered the air and fell harmlessly to the ground. The floor was slick with Boss Johnson's blood, but none of the Wraith team reacted. They were all focused on the four defenders—and wondering where the rest of the eight-man security force of Hochhaus was hiding.

For his part, Overwatch was simultaneously checking his weapons and scanning through the flak tower's surveillance cameras.

"Commander, four additional defenders on the floor above you," he said. "They are holding position. Team Juke is out, three minutes, thirty."

"Copy that," came the response from inside the flak tower. The commander's voice was slightly obscured by static and the echo of gunfire.

The Wraiths were now in position, firing in a set pattern, but random so the defenders could not anticipate who would be shooting next. They were too close to safely use explosives, so it was a standard gunfight.

Cross fired empty and ducked down to reload his SMG. Truck Miller immediately came up from cover to resume firing, but this action was anticipated by the Hochhaus defense. Mack was hit with a withering volley of Metal Storm bullets and his head simply evaporated in a pink mist. There was a stunned silence from all involved. A battlefield, by definition, is built on violence, but the sheer ferocity of the attack caught everyone off-guard. Now there were eight men in the room—four Wraiths and four Hochhaus – all ducked behind cover.

There was, perhaps, 30 seconds of silence as all eight men took the time to reload and let the echoes of gunfire drain away.

Suddenly, there was a voice over the Wraith comms.

"Commander," said Overwatch. "Get down."

Followed immediately by another voice.

"Chaf," announced Commander Bilkins from the support team.

All of the Wraiths immediately lay prone on the ground, protecting their weapons and electronics. Suddenly, the exterior door was flung inward, followed by soft "whump" sounds. There was a half-second delay and then the room exploded with sticky chaf. It resembled tiny pieces of confetti, or glitter, that filled the room. The small materials drifted to the ground, catching the four Hochhaus men completely off guard.

In fact, the chaf would attach to and jam the mechanics of the exposed weaponry. In an instant, the mighty Metal Storm AICW's were 13-pound hunks of metal, useful only as clubs. While the chaf was still drifting to the ground, the remainder of the Wraith assault force— including their commander—was up over the barricades and set upon the Hochhaus force with knives.

Bloodied and breathing hard from exertion, the four Wraith men stood, sheathed their knives, nodded their thanks to the support team, and took up position near the previously barricaded exit. The two commanders met briefly.

"Gettin' real tired of having to save your ass, Beef." Commander Bilkins grinned.

Commander Scott knelt to pick up his assault rifle and smiled.

"About a dozen more times and we should be even, Bilkins." Scott touched his ear to ensure that his receiver was properly seated after the action. "Overwatch, do you have eyes on the remaining Hochhaus force?"

Five of the support team took up position near the main door of this floor of the flak tower. Two of the men set about stowing the fallen Wraiths in thick, black Mylar bags. The remaining men formed up with the Wraiths as they prepared to storm the stairwell.

"Affirmative, Commander," Overwatch replied. "Four more men on the floor above you. Nearly the same set-up. Debris and barricades all around the floor. They are at the far wall. The scientists are in a panic room. Same floor."

Beef Scott nodded at the response and then to Bilkins.

"Copy that, Overwatch," he said. "We're Oscar Mike."

He walked over to his men.

"We're going up quietly. Stack up on the door." He turned to Bilkins. "Bangers? Then we go loud."

Bilkins nodded. The four Wraiths took point with Cross, Lugnuts, and Dandy moving silently up the stairs followed by their commander. As they had taken losses, they naturally and subconsciously moved to protect their leader. When they reached the second floor, they paused— two men on each side.

"Looks like they're getting antsy, sir," Overwatch said to the team, now patched into the Team Juke comms also.

"Copy that," Beef whispered into his throat mic. He gestured for each of his men to pull out a flashbang—or stun—grenade. They would stagger throwing four grenades into the room, blinding and disorienting the defensive force. Two of the Team Juke men had grenade launchers at the ready. They knew that as soon as they opened the stair door, they would face an aggressive volley of gunfire from four more AICWs.

A fifth man kicked open the door and dove out of the way. As expected, a brutal volley of gunfire erupted all around them. Reaching around the protection of the door jamb, Lugnuts tossed his flashbang into the room. It popped in a brilliant flash of light designed to blind and disorient an opposing force. The Metal Storm fire slowed as one or two of the men took cover. In order, the three other Wraiths also threw their flashbangs. With the enemy position in total disarray, the two Juke soldiers crouched at the doorway and fired two grenades each at the enemy position. There were four, almost simultaneous explosions— deafening in the enclosed space. The floor must have measured nearly 20 meters square, but the walls shook with the force of the four grenades.

Everyone's ears were ringing.

"All clear, Commander," Overwatch's voice came through slightly muffled. "Direct hit."

Scott nodded to his men who entered the room guns up. They were taking no chances and had each unholstered a fresh weapon that had been protected from the earlier chaf explosion. They cleared the room and formed up outside the panic room door. According to the intel, there were 12 scientists inside.

"You might not want to watch this," Commander Scott said to Bilkins, who then looked up at one of the surveillance cameras. "Hit it."

"Copy that," replied Overwatch.

Suddenly, there was a clunk deep inside the heavy steel door and then the entire fixture started to swing into the large room. The three Wraiths opened fire into the panic room as Alexander "Beef" Scott turned and walked away.

* *

Typically, the Wraith team would leave and allow the support team to extract whatever data they could before razing the structure to the ground. In this instance, the two teams blended together. As much as anything, it was a thank you to Team Juke for coming in and providing additional gunfire when the assault team needed it most. All-in-all, the 20-strong team made quick work of the flak tower research laboratory.

Much of the finished space of the tower was devoted to fabrication, storage, crew quarters, and a gym. There was only one floor that needed to be carefully examined.

"What the hell?" Cross Christianson muttered under his breath.

One entire wall of this floor was covered by a lighted whiteboard. On it was an explosion of drawings, equations, taped computer print-outs, and printed screen-grabs of hazy video. One section of the whiteboard was dedicated to drawings of various reptiles with humans sketched in for size comparisons. One particular drawing seemed to show a human inside a reptilian body. It was impossible to understand the goal and scope of the research that was being performed at this facility and the Wraith team would usually be long-gone before the cleaners even started their work.

Beef clapped Cross on the shoulder.

"Button it up, soldier."

Cross nodded.

"Yes, sir," he said and walked back to the task he was helping with. Twenty minutes later, the soldiers all exited the building and walked to the extraction point—each with a huge canvas bag full of recovered computers, binders, charts, and anything that could be salvaged.

They could all smell smoke from the burning facility.

CHAPTER EIGHT
THE DRONE PARTY

THEY ALL stood motionless in the airlock. It was a cramped space for this many people, but Damon realized it would only be an uncomfortable situation for a short time. There was a large digital countdown on the forward wall, right above the door to the outside. The countdown, right down to the font used, was mimicked on the HUD screen of his faceplate. He could feel his pulse pounding in his ears.

"Calm down," came the slightly synthetic but crystal clear voice of his friend Miles Lofton. "You're gonna be okay."

Damon looked to his right and saw Miles staring at him, smiling. Damon nodded his head in response. The new addition to the team sighed and felt perspiration break out on his upper lip. The rational side of his brain realized this was just an autonomic response—a stressful new situation. Otherwise, he noted that the temperature was slowly increasing in the small room—as evidenced by his HUD monitor— supposedly to get them acclimated to the outside research area. New temperature, slightly different air composition, different relative humidity, even, possibly, a slightly different atmosphere.

The countdown reached its short conclusion.

3. 2. 1.

The warning klaxons were loud, metallic sounds. As they started to go off, Cadey reached up and hit the large green button marked "Authorize." There was a two-second delay and the big steel door started to open.

"Whoa," Damon said.

* *

The memory appeared out of nowhere and seemingly cut from whole-cloth. Damon, really, had no idea where it had come from and what had sparked it. There were no familiar sights, sounds, or smells to trigger such an odd episode from his past. Perhaps, it was just the fact that he was walking next to Miles Lofton again. Perhaps it was contextually driven.

Perhaps it was something he had heard earlier in the day.

Save the planet.

They were in Berkeley, California, a decade ago. It was a bright, sunny, late-fall day in Northern California. Damon Butcher and Miles Lofton had few actual classes together, but they were roommates in a scholarship dorm and had become quick friends. They had met up for lunch and were walking back to a common area where they would part ways until the foosball tournament that would start prior to dinner.

What caught their eyes was a protest.

The University of California Berkeley has always been a hotbed of free-thinking and riled-up students. During Damon's time there, it seemed like there was some sort of rally or march or protest or event every week. This time, the peaceful protest included a couple dozen people milling about with signs. One folding buffet table filled with literature, manned by a single student. And one student with a megaphone, shouting a cadence.

Save The Planet, said the banner across the front of the information table.

"Jesus Christ soaked in butter," Miles said.

"Leave 'em alone," Damon said, smiling.

Miles hefted his backpack from his right shoulder to the left.

"No," he finally said. "How *else* are they going to learn?"

It was a 20-year-old blonde woman controlling the megaphone. She was wearing fashionable clothes that had been fashionably distressed. Her chanting started to break apart as Miles continued to approach her. He wore a friendly smile, but it was clear that he wasn't there to sign up for their cause. Three young men abandoned the picket-line and came to stand behind the blonde.

"Save what planet, exactly?" Miles said, still smiling broadly. He switched shoulders again. Damon stood a pace or so behind his friend, watching the show.

"The Earth, of course," she said. She was an economics major named Katie.

"My position is that the Earth is doing fine," he said. "Convince me otherwise."

Katie cleared her throat. Typically, she was always ready for a battle, but had somehow been thrown off her usual stance.

"We have pamphlets and brochures available right here," Katie said, gesturing to the table. "Feel free to take some and read them at your leisure."

Miles shook his head.

"I'm here right now, with you. You seem to be the leader of this group, so I assume you are well informed. Convince me that yours is a noble cause and my friend and I will join your group. We'll double the size of this event in an hour."

"Global warming is melting the polar ice caps and causing sea levels to rise," she said. "We will lose many islands, and coastlines around the planet will be forever changed."

Miles once again shook his head. The smile never left his face.

"A 2014 report by the Global Warming Policy Foundation published findings that global sea levels have been rising slowly for more than 10,000 years. They explicitly stated that there is no evidence that rising sea levels have anything to do with climate change."

"The polar icecaps are melting," Katie fired back. "Huge icebergs consistently break off Antarctica due to the violent climate change."

"I don't think so," Miles said. "Icebergs are calving from the Antarctic Peninsula, but this area only represents about two percent of the continent. It has consistently been reported in scientific journals that the interior of Antarctica has been getting colder—with the ice getting thicker."

All of the protesters had stopped and were watching this exchange. They were used to skeptics, and they were used to Katie and other members of the group winning their arguments.

"In 2013, the IPCC released data that showed that ocean temperatures were rising at an unprecedented rate due to global warming."

Miles shook his head for a third time.

"The IPCC used data largely generated from computer models. A computer model can't be a proof or an accurate prediction of anything. Scientific peers, using strictly observational data, agreed that the IPCC's projections were far too high." Lofton paused for a second. Katie, it seemed, was gearing up for a rebuttal. "Listen, you're doing good work. There're a lot of areas in which we need to improve. Our reliance on fossil fuels. The protection of poverty-stricken coastal communities.

Recycling. But, it's important to remember that this planet hates us. It keeps things in perspective."

"What the hell are you talking about?" she said.

"Earth is more than five billion years old and she has been experimenting since day one. Different environments. Different climates. Different species. We're simply the latest in a long line of dominant inhabitants. The Earth doesn't care about us and the idea of saving the planet is prideful in the extreme."

"We control our destiny," Katie fired back. "Our actions directly impact the environment. Our pollution. Our land use. Our waste."

"Do you know how many lightning strikes hit the planet's surface every second? One hundred. Every second. That's about three billion strikes per year. One thousand tornadoes rip across the United States each year. 20,000 earthquakes are recorded every year…with millions more falling below the data threshold."

He paused for a second and took one final step forward, closing the gap. The rest of the protesters were staring.

"We live on a violent, aggressive, ever-changing planet that was doing just fine before we arrived and will be doing just fine after our bones have turned to dust. You have a strong message, but it's founded in crap. Rhetoric. A PR machine that is fighting to justify its own means. Pick a specific problem and attack it. Road blow, for example. Or sinkhole detection methods. Or medical science. Don't try to save the planet—that's not for you to do. Try to improve one little aspect of your world."

* *

Ten years later, but 100 million years earlier, Damon Butcher smiled at the memory.

"1,500 active volcanoes around the world and only 500 have yet to erupt," he said under his breath, and continued to grin.

"What was that?" came a slightly metallic but still oddly clear voice. It was Lazlo Hollyfeld. Damon had read his dossier during his downtime while waiting for the mission to start. Mid-twenties. Tall, lanky build with abnormally large hands. Hollyfeld had attained three tech PhDs simultaneously. Two at MIT and one doing online coursework because he was bored.

"Talking to myself," Damon answered. "Just a memory from my college days." Miles didn't respond over comms, but Butcher was certain he had heard a chuckle.

The team stood in a vaguely defined group about 10 meters outside the huge steel door that protected Gamma Complex—the abbreviated version of O221 in the Cretaceous. Miles was reading something on the wrist-attached computer pad on his left arm. He finished reading, tapped the screen a few times, and the mission data appeared on everyone's wrist pad. A single image appeared on their faceplate HUDs, replaced by a second and a third. They all dropped down to thumbnail size along the left edge of their vision.

Flowers.

"Today's mission should be an easy one," Miles said over the group communications net. "No animals. Just plants. Specifically these three. We need two of each of these three flowers. There's a study about threat response that we need to populate."

"Walk to the end of the driveway and back," Calvin Brunarski added and Miles nodded. Calvin was a stocky man—dark hair and dark complexion. He was late middle-aged and the most senior member of the team—at least as far as age and seniority with Allied Genetics was concerned. He wore a black Fu Manchu-style mustache and would never admit to darkening it with hair dye.

"Exactly," Miles said. "The challenge is 30 minutes. We split off into teams of two. Shouldn't take all that long to find the six specimens. We should have a longer project tomorrow, but this is more to get Damon's feet wet."

Everyone nodded. There was no hazing ritual at Allied Genetics, but a new recruit's first adventure into the deep past was usually a short one. They were very aware of the potentially overwhelming experience.

"Great," Cadey Park said, tapping Damon on the shoulder. "It's my turn in the rotation. I'll show him the ropes."

* *

Cadey Park was 30 years old but, perhaps stereotypically, you couldn't guess her age by looking at her. She had defected from North Korea in her teens as a National Math Champion and had advanced her knowledge through various degrees in American colleges. She took on cryptozoology as a hobby and, according to Lofton's hand-written note on the dossier he had given Damon, she knew more about the subject than Damon himself—who had an advanced degree.

"So," Cadey said. "Precision Robotics, huh?"

The six-person excursion had divided up into three smaller teams. They were each looking for the different targets, but there was no competition. Ultimately, the goal was to finish up and head back to base for an evening off.

"Yep." Damon nodded. "I was heading up the theoretical biometrics department and doing some cross-training in programming."

"What brought you to our little corner of the universe?"

Damon shrugged.

"I knew Miles from college." He paused for a moment, running his thickly gloved hand across a two-meter-tall shrub top. "Plus a raise and the promise of high adventure."

Cadey nodded.

"That'll get you every time." She paused for a moment as both of them read the information on their HUD. One of the teams had grabbed a set of plants. "I did some consulting work for Precision a few years ago. Not a bad organization."

"Yeah. What kind of work did you do?" Damon asked, and then exclaimed as his HUD highlighted one of the plants noted in their excursion documents.

Cadey reached down to uproot it and slide it into a protective bag.

"They were doing some research on drone technology. Very hush, hush." She stood up and clipped the bag to a metal ring on the outer edge of her right leg. Standing, she made a thumb gesture to her back, over her shoulder, indicating her bag. "It's a hobby of mine, so I helped them out."

Damon made a move to look at her back, but she had turned away and stepped through some foliage.

"Got another," she called over the faceplate microphone.

Just as quickly, Damon saw his own HUD light up with the six plant images—two for each of the three various plants—five of them now had red Xs across the image, indicating that they had been collected already. Soon, he heard Emi Tolliver's voice over his speakers.

"Got the last one," she said. Emi was another young, female researcher on Lofton's team. She was in her late 20s and kept her head shaved. Language, it seemed, was her hobby as she had degrees from around the world and spoke three languages fluently. Born in Boston, her first language experiment was to completely remove her accent.

As Damon recalled this note from her dossier, he also noticed that Cadey spoke with only a hint of an accent. He realized that she had spent the first half of her life—the formative years of language—in her native North Korea. There should have been some vestiges of an accent. He was only picking them up on random words.

"I was noticing your accent," he said as she emerged from the small group of trees. "Or, rather, your lack of one."

Cadey nodded as if this was a discussion she had been through on numerous occasions.

"During undergrad, I sought out friends who were from accent-neutral parts of the U.S. Northern California. The central Midwest. Places like that. I worked to emulate their speech."

It was Damon's turn to nod.

"So, you have a drone in your backpack?"

"Yes she does," came Miles Lofton's voice over the plate speakers. And, just like that, all six members of the research team were back in the same area forming a natural semi-circle. "It comes in handy, sometimes, when we're trying to peek around certain corners. You know. To stay safe."

"Can I try?" Damon said, turning from Miles to Cadey after the question was asked...seeking permission from both at the same time. Certain that he didn't want to offend anyone. "I've never actually flown one."

Cadey looked to Miles who made a dramatic motion of checking the non-existent watch on his wrist. Everyone had a small box of text data in the bottom-right corner of the HUD that, oddly, expanded when they looked at it, and contained the current time at O221, the local temperature, and relative humidity.

"Sure. Five minutes."

* *

It felt like someone had taken a video game controller, broken it in half, and added a computer tablet in between the two handles. Damon held the controller comfortably. It was a bit heavy, but rested easily in the palms of his hands. His left thumb controlled the elevation and his right thumb controlled lateral movement. The left trigger controlled the zoom of the camera and the right trigger controlled lateral speed. As a lifelong gamer, the control interface was intuitive and easy. Within moments, he was a pro.

He watched the drone zoom up and away from the group and began to familiarize himself with the camera screen.

Damon was flanked by Miles and Cadey. The other three researchers busied themselves with other projects. Calvin was cataloging each of the six plant specimens, all laid out on the ground in front of him. Emi was tracking a dinosaur—noted as BPS-N651—and snapping photos of him. It was the size of a large dog, a deep brown color, with a spiked tail jutting out twice the length of his body. Lazlo stood by the airlock door, running various environmental tests, gauging air composition.

Cadey leaned in closer to Damon and started pointing out various elements of the display.

"Elevation in meters, remaining battery, distance from base—which is you—and effective range, horizon indicator."

Damon was grinning broadly.

"Yup," he said. "Just like a pretty basic flight simulator."

He was manipulating the device this way and that, watching the screen like a child with a new toy. The image and the metrics all blended into one simultaneous input. Damon soon began to attempt new button/control interface combinations. Suddenly, the screen went all topsy-turvy and Cadey jerked in reaction.

"What happened?"

"Yeager Roll." Damon smiled.

As the screen image stabilized and the horizon once again indicated level, a quarter of the right side of the screen went black. Damon frowned.

"What's that all about?" he asked.

Cadey furrowed her brow and looked at the distance and coordinates.

"That's a geo-error," she said, Miles also leaning in closer. "There are some spaces that are blocked from our equipment. Some sort of electromagnetic interference. We have a team at 221 trying to clear it, but it's a pretty consistent error."

Damon swung the camera around directly toward the error. Slowly, as if it was panning from right to left, the entire screen went black.

"Hmm," Damon said to himself. He didn't turn to look, but spoke to Miles.

"Did you try—?" he started.

"Yeah," Miles answered, assuming the first solution Damon would have reached. "We tried to calibrate with Gamma Complex's equipment."

"What if you—?" he started again.

"It's no use to feed the uplink right into the faceplate," Miles said. "There's not a stable way to boost the signal without frying capacitor-G."

"Hmm."

Damon started to lower the elevation of the drone, slowly. The screen remained black until it became static and then cleared. Damon halted the descent. According to the display, the drone was about 10 meters above the surface, looking at dense foliage another five meters directly in front of it. He cocked his head sideways and began to spin the drone in a 360-degree movement. Directly behind the drone was a huge clearing. When he came back and faced the foliage, he paused.

"Okay," Butcher said.

"Let's wrap it up," Miles said, tapping his imaginary watch. The rest of the team heard this and began finishing their individual projects.

"Hang on," Damon said.

Cadey leaned in and looked at the screen.

"I learned this from a video game."

Slowly, the drone began to ascend and pull backward at the same time. Damon increased pressure on the analog trigger to slowly zoom the little camera. As the drone backed up and elevated, the zoom kept the trees clearly in focus. Soon, he reached the level where the static assaulted the screen.

"Okay," Damon said, leaning in toward the screen. He continued his backward ascent. The drone cleared the static and, instead of going black, the screen remained active.

"Oh. Wow," Cadey said. "I need to play more video games."

Damon reached the tops of the trees and they found themselves looking into a clearing much like the one that was at the rear of the little drone.

"Holy shit," Damon said and paused the ascent of the drone. He zoomed the camera in full.

"It's a road," Cadey said, breathlessly.

* *

The five members of the expedition team crowded around Damon. They were all staring at the screen. Miles had forgotten about his fake countdown.

Through the short prairie grasses was a clear road—an artificial path. A dead-straight, slightly indented path that ran for just more than 100 meters and disappeared behind another huge clump of trees.

"I don't know what I'm seeing," Damon said, maneuvering the drone back and forth, testing the geo-error area. Suddenly, an area snapped into focus. It was hard to accurately estimate due to the height of the drone, but a section of hard, smooth pavement appeared. It was a chunk of ground five by five meters square. Even though nature had reclaimed the vast majority of this area, a small section remained visible. It was clearly artificial.

"I don't think we should be seeing this," Calvin said from behind Miles.

Miles turned his head to look at the team. Cadey, in one smooth motion, pressed a small thumb drive into the side of the control panel and pushed an icon labeled "record local." Damon looked at her out of the corner of his eye, but didn't react.

"Let's pack it up," Miles said, facing away from the display screen. "We'll discuss this at the next team meeting. For now, we have loads of data to prepare."

Cadey, again, in a quick motion, pulled the thumb drive out of the machine and the "record" icon, previously lit, went dark. All told, she had recorded roughly 20 seconds of data.

Miles turned to look at Damon.

"Alright," he said. "Let's bring it down."

"You got it," Damon said, nodding. Finally, he cast a sideways glance at Cadey Park who hefted an eyebrow as both a challenge to say something and an imploration to stay quiet. "Comin' down."

CHAPTER NINE
THE ROAD

IT WASN'T quite a conference room and it wasn't quite a break room. It wasn't quite a living space. Lofton's expedition team had found a little-used room that was somehow in the middle of all of these functions. There was a small kitchenette in the corner and a slim refrigerator full of soda, snacks, and bottled water. Of course, the dominant feature of the room was the large circular table in the center.

Miles Lofton sat in one of the Spartan cloth and wood chairs. He had a legal pad flipped open in front of him with a variety of pens at the ready.

"But our debriefings are typically in 206," Calvin Brunarski said.

And he was right.

Most often, the expedition team would discuss their latest excursion in the large, official conference room in MV206. They would compare notes and discuss anything that needed to be fixed or addressed by management. In this instance, Miles steered them into the first open room.

"You're right," Miles said. "But since this is more of an anomaly, I wanted to get into a room and talk about it ASAP without having to schedule our regular area."

Calvin nodded.

"Okay," he said and looked around the table, still nodding, to gauge any dissent. There was none.

He sat next to Miles. Cadey Park sat on the other side of Miles with Emi directly next to her. Damon and Lazlo rounded out the seating.

"It looked like a road," Emi Tolliver said as she rubbed her right hand up across the crown of her head. She, at once, hated and relished the feel of the stubble there. Time to shave.

Miles nodded his head.

"That's what it *looked* like," he said. "I agree. But I caution you all to fall into the trap of matrixing."

Damon nodded in reply. He had heard of this phenomenon.

"I don't get it," Lazlo said.

Cadey was leaning forward on her elbows, chin resting in the palm of her right hand.

"Matrixing is when the brain tries to make sense of its surrounding by arranging random objects into a recognizable pattern," she said. "People who see faces in wood grain. Or puppies in clouds." She paused for a moment. "Miles is suggesting that we didn't actually see a road, but disparate elements that arranged themselves to resemble a road in our brains. Right?"

"Exactly," Miles said. "It's a perceptive trick to assume that straight lines and right angles don't appear in nature. They're there. All the time."

"I'm not sure of what we hope to accomplish here," Damon said. "Not to speak out of turn, but, why don't we just go out and take a look in person?"

Calvin and Miles shook their heads at the same time. Calvin spoke first.

"First of all, an unsanctioned trip is against the rules. These things are carefully planned and scheduled. Company resources and all that. These trips aren't free. Second, there is the added problem of us looking into a geographic lock. That zone was off limits to us for any number of reasons. Dangerous predators. Volcanic activity. Heck. Residual toxic waste from a bygone meteor shower. For whatever the reason, the company decided that area was not to be explored."

"Couldn't have said it better myself," Miles said.

There was silence around the table. The implications of a super-ancient civilization were huge.

"It sure looked like a road," Emi said again. This time resting the palms of her hands flat on the table top. She looked like a teenager who was just told she couldn't go to the mall with her friends.

Miles shrugged.

"Look," he said. "There's no use for prediction without fully exploring the area." He paused. "We'd have to put a team together consisting of engineers, geologists, and us. Probably a few soldiers, too, in case things got weird. Let's put this whole discussion on hold until I've had a chance to talk to the boss. Maybe we can plan an excursion. But don't get your hopes up."

* *

"They found it."

After adjourning the meeting of the expedition team, Miles went directly to Britta Vragi's office. He was comically breathless after jogging from one end of the facility to the other. She motioned for him to sit down and compose himself before beginning the interrogation.

"Found *what*?" Britta said from behind her planet-sized desk.

"The road," Miles said as he slicked back the sweat from his forehead into the crown of his head, matting down his hair. "In the block zone. They were looking past the trees with a drone and saw the road."

Britta nodded.

"Who?"

"Today's expedition team. Brunarski, Hollyfeld, Park, Tolliver, and Butcher."

"Butcher?" she said, furrowing her brow. "The new guy?"

Miles nodded.

"He was the one piloting the drone."

Britta frowned at Miles, who tried to somehow dissolve into the leather chair and become invisible.

"Anything else?"

"Did they find anything else? No," Miles said. "I saw that they had seen the road and I shut down the expedition. Brought them back for debriefing."

Britta finally nodded.

"Okay, good work," she said. "That's good. I'll need to review any documentation. Did Calvin fill out a report?" Miles was shaking his head in response. "Okay, good. Any recordings?"

Miles paused.

"There was the drone video feed," he said. "But it doesn't automatically record."

"Sure. Okay. Wipe it anyway. Actually. Wait. Bring it to me and I'll wipe it myself."

She paused for a moment and Miles stood to leave. He stopped.

"Something wrong?"

"I think they're going to want to go back. Have another look."

"Pretty sure that's not going to happen," Britta said.

Miles nodded.

"I know," he said. He continued to stand rooted to the spot.

"Stall them," Britta said, sighing. "We'll come up with something official-sounding. Get me the drone control and I'll discuss the matter with my superiors."

Miles Lofton finally took his leave of the room. Britta immediately leaned forward and pressed a button on her phone.

"We've got a problem," she said into the receiver.

* *

Damon stared at the terrarium and let his mind wander. He was still new to this team—less than 20 hours ago, he was gainfully employed by Precision Robotics—and wanted to observe and fit in. The problem, though, was that he knew Miles and could read him like a book. What had been the actual purpose of that meeting? A debriefing? But, of what? They didn't discuss the road or the potential implications of a super-ancient society. What had Miles actually said?

Don't think about it. Don't ask about it.

As Damon left the meeting room, he saw his old friend hustle down a long hallway, presumably to talk to his boss about the matter. Brittany? Something.

He exhaled and crossed his arms against his chest. He was staring blankly at one particular plant. It was about two feet high with yellow, spiked protrusions along the base that gradually decreased in size as they climbed up the stalk. It had not flowered yet, but he could see the orangish bulbs at the end of the bigger stems. In contrast to the deep green color of the stalk and leaves, he felt the flowers would be beautiful.

Suddenly, something caught his eye in his periphery. It was a huge centipede—easily a foot long. It was black along the back with a yellow diamond pattern to match its yellow legs. It scuttled from under the mulch base of the enclosure, up a tree, and down the other side. Damon couldn't tell if Allied Genetics had intentionally brought the enormous insect into the plant display or it had hatched there. Either way…

"That's probably…*not* a good idea," Damon said quietly to himself.

"What's that?" Cadey Park asked. She had silently sidled up next to him and was watching the same scene he was.

"I, the…" He raised his right hand to point at the centipede but it had disappeared again. "Nothing."

They stood silently for a moment, the gentle whoosh of the HVAC system the only sound. People were moving to and fro throughout the corridor, but everything seemed quiet. Surreal. They stood side by side, staring into the glass enclosure. They might have both been looking for the giant, ancient centipede. They were both certainly trying to figure out what to say next.

It was finally Cadey who broke the silence. She cleared her throat and started talking without looking at Damon.

"The United States thinks it's old, but on a global civilization level, it's still very young. Young and kinda dumb. Like an awkward teenager at her first boy-girl party. Dumb teenagers tend to do things they think are smart or clever, but are generally neither."

Damon turned his head and looked at the young researcher. *She probably knows more than you*, the note had said. He inhaled and exhaled deeply.

"Take technology, for example. Things advance at different rates. Things are ignored. Things go intentionally unnoticed."

Cadey paused for a minute and coughed politely, quietly. It was almost a whisper behind a balled-up right hand.

"I lost my train of thought," she said.

Damon didn't believe her for some reason. He couldn't explain it, but he had the sudden inclination that she was trying to dumb-down her thought process.

"Now, listen," he started, but she held up a hand.

"At Michigan State University, a 200-year-old college in the Midwestern United States, there's a building in the linguistics neighborhood. The Brouwer Building. It's eight stories up and three down. On the lowest sub-level sits a computer. An ancient Amiga. The hardware's been upgraded so that it's Internet-capable."

"Okay."

"Yeah. It sits in this little storage locker, powered up, connected to the Internet. There's one document stored there. It's a 47-page master's thesis by a long-forgotten student. Joe, something. Stanwick, I think." She waved her hand absently. "*Slang as Regional Fashion − The Conundrum of the Synantonym.* You actually have to jump through several odd hurdles to get to it. But if you manage to get to this particular document stored on this particular computer in this particular building, the computer will wake up and you can read the paper. When you, as the end user, clicks off the page, the computer goes back to sleep and just waits. This document is not found anywhere else on the web. It's not in a library. Some say it was written and stored there as some sort of thought experiment. In any event, this is probably the first example of the deep web. Non-indexed data that can only be reached if you know how to reach it."

She paused again and furrowed her brow. After a moment of silence, Damon cleared his throat. He was still looking into the terrarium, but not really looking at anything.

"That's interesting."

Cadey nodded.

"I've always thought so. I've always wanted to take a field trip and just look at it. This bizarre little computer hiding from the rest of the world. Kind of. Always ready to be found, though."

"I'm curious as to why you told me that," Damon said, finally turning to look at her.

Cadey nodded. She was nearly a foot shorter than Damon and had to lean her head back slightly to look him in the eye.

"Ice breaker," she said. "We need to review that video footage. But we can't do it here. But we have to do it here. Right?"

Damon continued to gaze at her while Cadey turned her head to look back into the plant display. He had the sense that she was letting him put it together. For some reason. He was in no mood for puzzles or mind games.

He yawned. And it dawned on him.

"You have a secret workstation here in the building."

Cadey nodded.

"Yup. It was one of the first things I did when I got here. Totally off the Anvil Canyon grid, but still very powerful. It's the only place we can safely watch the drone video."

Damon looked around the hallway. He recognized no one.

"Lead the way," he said.

* *

Half a planet away, Alexander Scott strode through the open door of his commanding officer's headquarters and let it close behind him. Scott was one of the highest ranking field commanders for the Wraiths—the assault force often employed by Sergott Solutions when they had a serious client with a serious problem. Originally growing up on a ranch in Texas earned Scott the military call sign "Beef," one that had followed him his entire career.

It was a ranch in name only as his family had long abandoned being cattle-herders. Drill sergeants, however, didn't much care for family details.

Beef snapped off a perfunctory salute and addressed his commanding officer, Clay Reed.

"We have a problem, sir."

Reed nodded and leaned forward in his chair.

"At ease. Sit," Reed said. "I've read the mission debrief. Intel was bad."

In general, Scott preferred to remain standing, but sat in one of the two red leather chairs that faced Reed's desk. As if on cue, there was a knock at the now-closed door. It opened and another Wraith commander came in.

Rick "Ahab" Everson was of similar age and reputation to Scott. He saluted and sat next to his opposite number in front of the large desk.

"Sir." He nodded and turned to the man seated next to him. "Scott."

Scott nodded in reply.

"As you say, sir. Bad intel. They had advanced weaponry that hadn't been mentioned anywhere, as well as hardened defensive measures."

Clay was silent. He looked down at a thick file folder that rested in the center of his desk blotter. Opened it, scanned a couple pages, and closed it again.

"I agree," he finally said, seemingly addressing both men. "And it will be rectified. I've made the necessary notations in the file." He paused. "Now, for new business. We were commissioned for three total gags against Allied Genetics targets. Here is the third. Back to Europe for you, Beef. You'll be running the mission together. Ultimate oversight directly from this office, but you'll pair up in the field. One face. One voice. Clear?"

"Yes, sir."

"Crystal."

"Good," Clay said. "I should also mention that the client is preparing a fourth mission. This might also be a dual effort. Details forthcoming."

He looked at the two men, giving them just a moment to voice any concerns. No objections were raised and Clay Reed glanced back down to paperwork on his desk.

"Dismissed."

* *

It wasn't surprising that she led him into an area that he hadn't been yet. Was it true that he'd only been an employee of Allied Genetics for 24 hours?

That can't be right, Damon thought.

The corridors became less and less crowded the more turns they made. Finally, Cadey stopped in front of a door marked "Custodial Access." She made a great show of looking down at the clipboard she was carrying—a prop she brought with her from a storage closet just outside the terrarium—and then opened the door like she had a schedule to keep.

"Jesus," Damon said under his breath and followed her in.

The door hissed shut on its pneumatic hinge. They were standing in a narrow corridor. She glanced briefly over her right shoulder and strode off down the corridor. Damon had to hurry to keep up with her.

It looked like a maintenance corridor—akin to a wet wall in a large building. It was just wide enough to wind around the outer perimeter of this floor of Objekt 221. There were access panels at regular intervals and numerous computer terminals that seemed to be monitoring various aspects of the structure. From HVAC to water pressure, Damon noted numerous different systems in play.

There was a left turn and then a right and Cadey stopped at a door. One of the few doors they had passed in the area.

The paint on the door was faded, red and written in Cyrillic script. Damon could read: Avtorizovannyy personal. Authorized personnel. Cadey pulled a key from a tiny pocket in her blue jeans and opened the door.

"Home away from home," Cadey said.

It was a little room—basically a two-by-two meter square. There was a folding chair, folded, leaned up against the far corner from the door. She flipped a light switch as the door closed behind them. A single bulb hanging from the center of the ceiling came on. It was an industrial-type fixture in a room otherwise devoid of fixtures. There was a stack of random binders, small boxes, and even a crisply folded work shirt. Cadey bent down, reached behind this stack, and pulled out a laptop computer. She unfolded the chair, sat down in front of it, and snapped open the dark gray computer.

She arched her back and pulled the small USB drive out of the same pocket that had the room key. She felt along the right side of the laptop and plugged the device in. After a brief moment of whirring and grinding, a generic media player popped up on the screen.

"Okay," she said as Damon sat next to her cross-legged. "Here we go."

The video played in its entirety. It was 11 seconds long. For 10 and a half seconds, they watched the drone pulling away with what the team was calling "the road" in the top, center of the screen. The final half-second was a burst of static and wavy lines that obscured the image as Cadey had yanked the USB drive from the drone control's port.

"It looks like a road," Cadey said.

Damon shrugged.

"I suppose," he said. "I'm starting to think along the same lines as what Miles said about matrixing. Maybe we're just imposing order on random images."

It was Cadey's turn to shrug, then she pointed at the screen as she instructed the video to run on a continuous loop.

"I think I'd be more inclined to agree with you if it didn't look like the environment had been engineered," she said. Cadey pointed at the screen and ran the tip of her right index finger across a line on the laptop. "Right here. These indentations."

"Yeah. I can see that. But you gotta admit that strange things happen in nature. Things that seem engineered, but are natural formations." He thought for a moment. "Depending on the terrain, many trees grow perfectly perpendicular to the ground. Sodium chloride often forms perfect cubes. Hell, the basalt columns of Giant's Causeway look like manufactured pillars but they are a natural volcanic formation."

Cadey nodded. She was pursing her lips.

"I understand what you're saying," she said. "And if it was just a straight clearing for a few hundred meters…sure. I just can't get past how much it looks like this was built. This was engineered."

The video ran three more times with the two room occupants watching in silence. The light flickered once in its small metal cage in

71

the center of the ceiling. When the recording started to run forward a fourth time, Damon leaned forward.

"Wait a second," he said. Cadey turned to look at him. "Can we do this...um...advance the video frame-by-frame?"

"Probably," she said. "This is a fairly simple program, but it would make sense to have that option."

She paused the playback and started to move the cursor around the screen looking at various options and settings.

"Yeah. Here we go."

The video started to play again, but with the pop, pop, pop jerk of one frame at a time. It almost looked like stop-motion animation.

"Right toward the end," Damon said. "Before the glitch."

Cadey advanced the playback almost all the way forward. She pulled the cursor forward until the 10.5 second mark and let it play. There were five stop-motion images of the road and then sudden static. The static was replaced by wavy lines indicating digital interference. The lines jumped and danced and a clear image emerged for only one frame before disappearing into a wave of static.

They both leaned forward.

"Can you...?" Damon said.

"Already on it," Cadey answered.

She paused the playback and rolled it backward two, three frames. The clear image that was only visible for a quarter of a second froze and filled the screen.

They saw the road begin to curve away to the left, toward the bottom of the image. Something was just emerging into the frame—at the very top of the screen.

"What the fuck is that?" Damon said, squinting.

"It's a..." Cadey started. "Oh shit." Her eyes widened.

"It's a building," Damon said.

CHAPTER TEN
THE MOUNTAIN

BUILT ON the strength of back-breaking slave labor, some of the Third Reich's most impressive military works have a dark history—haunted by the ghosts of hundreds of thousands of unwilling participants. As the tide of the war began to turn in 1943, the Nazi regime decided to centralize most of their operations. Their master plan: Project Riese. *The Giant.*

The Owl Mountains are one of Poland's oldest ranges, stretching along the Czech border. As a largely inaccessible terrain with a dense spruce forest, it's no wonder the German army identified the region as a potential stronghold. Project Riese would be a massive undertaking—an underground complex carved right into the side of the mountain.

Ten of the tunnel complexes have been excavated, but only a portion have truly been explored. Only a small percentage of the underground facilities were completed to any degree with very few meters reinforced with concrete and steel support beams.

The 11th facility was located nearly five miles away—connected to the complex by a rail line—and doesn't appear on any surveys. Complex Ksiaz was the first started and last abandoned. That section of land was quietly purchased in the late 1980s by a private consortium. While remaining under the control of a single entity for decades, work was slowly completed. In 2010, the ribbon-cutting ceremony on the Allied Genetics facility—known internally as Rainier Mesa—was quietly held nearly a quarter of a mile underground.

* *

As the combined Wraith assault teams made their final gear checks in their big Chinook transport copter, the two commanders engaged in some friendly banter.

"So, we'll be Team Alpha and you'll be Team Bravo," Alex Scott said, smiling.

"No dice, Beef," replied Rick "Ahab" Everson, hefting an eyebrow.

The two men were of similar age and experience level, but they couldn't be more different physically. Scott was slim and wiry. He had blond hair and fair features. He grew up in Texas, but was mentally a California boy—embracing the surfer culture. Ahab Everson was a bruiser. A battering ram. A human tank. Standing nearly 6'5" and tipping the scales at 280, his fatigues had to be custom fit. Dark hair, a dark beard, and scars up and down the knotted muscles of his arms.

"Okay," Beef decided to try again. "We'll be Team Gold and you'll be Team Silver."

Many of the men in the hold of the Boeing helicopter were on the common team communication line. They were laughing.

"If you are Gold, then my team is Titanium," Ahab countered.

"Hmm," Alex said. "Won't work. Too many syllables. It might confuse the radio operator. One, Two? Legends, Leaders? Upper, Lower? Just spitballin' here."

Ahab laughed and clapped Beef on the shoulder blade. His hand nearly covered a quarter of the man's back.

"Everything you suggest implies a primary and secondary function. A number one team and a support. You have to change your mindset, Beef." Ahab squared his shoulders and hooked his thumbs in the waistband of his pants. All 10 men were listening, now, including the pilots. "Pick two of the same thing. Sure there might be personal preferences that puts one above the other, but two types of guns. Two types of trees. Of cars. Two colors. How about that?"

"Hmm," Alex said for the second time. "Like Team Charger and Team Challenger?"

"There you go," Ahab said, shooting him a winning smile. "You are Team Charger. We are Team Challenger."

There was a short pause as Beef considered this.

"Charger. I'm definitely gonna forget that shit."

* *

Many of the Wraiths knew each other across teams, either through actually working together or by reputation. There were 11 men on the combined assault force, including the two commanders. There was an offsite mission overwatch currently maneuvering a military drone to do a fly-by over the Owl Mountain property.

The men were tracking through the forest, stalking toward what their intelligence indicated would be the least-guardable entrance.

"All clear," Overwatch radioed in from his remote location.

"Copy that," Ahab responded. He looked toward Scott who was walking immediately to his right. "You *smell* that?"

Beef was silent for a few steps, breathing deeply. In through the nose, out through the mouth. Finally, he nodded.

"I'm getting smoke," he said, glancing around. "Not seeing any bonfires."

Ahab nodded in response.

"Right."

On the far side of the flanking formation, two men, reunited for the first time since college ROTC, were talking off mic. Lonny "Doc" Watley and Ben "Cross" Christianson did their undergrad together at Purdue, went into the service after graduation and were split up after basic.

"So," Doc said, carefully stepping over a fallen branch. "Are we looking to find hidden Nazi gold or something?"

"What?" Cross replied, not looking at his old friend.

"These tunnels. Project Riese. Don't you watch the History Channel? The rumor that the Nazis wheeled a train full of gold in here and walled it off before the end of the war. Ten billion dollars in gold. You never heard about this?"

Ben simply shook his head.

"You think Allied found it first?" Doc asked. "Maybe that's how they got so rich. Found an assload of gold hidden in the mountains. Talk about your initial investment."

"I suppose," Ben said. "They're the bad guys, right? The bad guys never seem to have a problem with funding."

"I suppose that's true, too," Doc said.

They were approaching the ventilation shaft.

"Do you smell smoke?" Doc asked.

"Okay. Charger on the left. Challenger on the right. Form up," the instructions came from Ahab Everson as the two commanders split their teams up into two, one on each side of the ventilation shaft.

The men all paused. Commander Scott pulled off his right glove and held his bare hand up to the mesh covering of the ventilation shaft. Two men—one on each side of the portal—began unbolting the big cover. Alex pulled his hand back and looked at his opposite number on the other team.

"It's warm," he said. "Warmer than it probably should be."

Ahab nodded.

"Still smelling smoke," he said. "I'm getting a real *scorched earth* feeling here." He paused for a minute and then spoke into his throat mic. "Overwatch, how many in the facility?"

There was a slight pause as Overwatch—a young specialist sitting comfortably in mission control in front of two computers, three monitors, and a laptop screen connected directly to a series of military-grade drones—tapped away at his primary workstation.

"Eight researchers logged in this evening, sir," he said. "Eight security. I'm showing all internal security is disabled. All door locks are disengaged. None of the workers have logged back out."

"Has the remote uplink come through?"

In the darkness of his tech room, Overwatch nodded in response.

"Yes, sir, 98 percent uplink," Overwatch said. "It's coming through just now."

There was a pause. The two men had removed the final set of bolts from the cover. The ventilation gridwork was being held in place by gravity and a little rust.

"Um," Overwatch said. "I have no video, sir."

"No video?" Beef asked.

"No, sir," mission control said. "I have a strong uplink, but I'm receiving no signal. Scratch that, sir. I'm receiving static from two surveillance cameras. Completely dark on the other six."

Thousands of miles away, the two commanders looked at each other.

"They went dark waiting for us?" Beef said.

"Or it's destruction protocol," Ahab responded. "They knew we were coming and burned the place down rather than have us take it."

Beef thought for a moment and then nodded his head.

"I got a bad feeling about this," he said.

* *

Utter devastation.

There were probably three miles of winding tunnels that made up the Rainier Mesa facility—the 11th secret underground complex buried beneath the Owl Mountains. As the two Wraith teams entered the facility through the oversized air vent and split up to neutralize the hostile force, they noticed two things.

One: there was no hostile force.

Two: the facility had been incinerated.

The walls were caked in soot and the polished concrete floor throughout the facility was covered with ash. The air was so thick with the lingering smell of smoke that the men all wore respirators.

"Scorched earth," said Doc Watley into his microphone as he and Team Charger explored the west wing of the facility.

"Clearly they didn't want to lose any more data after losing two facilities," Ahab spoke to the team at large. "Our mission parameters only slightly change. We need to verify that the facility is clear of hostiles and call in the information extraction team to see if there's anything to salvage."

The two teams continued to work apart from each other. Charger to the west and Challenger to the east. They would advance on a room, enter and clear it, and then move on to the next.

"Also curious about the 16 bodies that clocked in for the evening, but never clocked back out," Beef said as his team approached the farthest point on the east of the facility.

There was a general silence punctuated by a few grunts in the affirmative. A sudden intake of air, however, broke the silence as the final room in this section was reached.

"Oh, wow," said Wilson "Dandy" Reid. "Sir, there is definite scarring on the door and surrounding area, but it appears to taper off. Metal hinges and door latch appear to be unharmed." There was a nameplate on the high center of the door. Dandy reached up and rubbed his hand across the laser-carved letters. *S. Mathias.*

The Challenger team was standing in several puddles of wet foam. While the door to S. Mathias's office was slightly damaged, the opposite wall of the hallway was virtually untouched. Wet, and a little slimy, but untouched.

"Copy that," Beef said. He looked up, the helmet-mounted light illuminating the ceiling. "I have an undamaged sprinkler right here," he said. "Foam fire retardant on the floor. They must have deactivated the sprinkler system and set fire to the facility. This one, unfortunately for them, still did its job."

"We couldn't *be* that lucky," Ahab said over the team channel.

"Breaching, sir," Dandy said as the two forward men were in position. There was a sharp crack as the locking mechanism was destroyed. The door groaned as it was pushed open against the char and soot that had made its way to this final room.

"Whoa," said Beef as the team's flashlights played across the interior of the office. It was crowded and disheveled, but untouched by the fire that had destroyed the rest of the facility.

"We're on our way," Ahab said.

* *

The data extraction team was on their way to the Owl Mountain complex. Everything else in the facility was a charred mess. S. Mathias's office, however, had been untouched by the destruction due to a faulty tamper job or an aggressively efficient fire-retardant system—depending on the perspective.

They had guessed correctly from the main hallway. It was truly an office, albeit nondescript. There were no architectural details save for the door and two vents—a heat register and a return vent. There was a desk, a large bookcase, a combination whiteboard and corkboard on one wall, a small table, and a guest chair in the corner. All told, the office was a 3.5-meter square.

With the support team en route, most of the Wraith squad was manning the entrances/exits of the hidden facility. Two men were sweeping for booby-traps that might have been missed on the initial examination. The two commanders, however, remained in the office. They were making small talk and nosing around the room to pass the time.

"So," Ahab said, flipping through a stack of paper and dropping it back on the small desk. "Initial assessment is what?" Alex "Beef" Scott had his back turned to his co-commander. He was studying the corkboard and the various bits and pieces that get attached to them. A calendar with notes about birthdays and anniversaries. A postcard from a friend on vacation. A letter, opened and returned to the envelope, presumably to be replied to. In and around these personal touches, though, was a litter of important business notes. A memo with bits of text highlighted about new security cards. A diagram of the facility. A slip of paper, folded against itself and hidden behind another paper. It was a list of passwords to various company systems.

Beef shrugged.

"Not sure," he said, turning back to face his partner. "It certainly doesn't seem too serious. My first thought was that it was a storage facility. Possibly data mining." He shrugged again and added another, "Not sure."

Something, however, caught his eye.

He leaned down to a small table that was desk-adjacent. On it sat a small, ancient, bubble-jet printer. It was stacked high with books and manuals and black binders. Perhaps that was the reason that a few pages sat on the printer tray, ignored. Beef picked the small stack up and scanned through it.

"Uh oh," he said.

Ahab turned and closed the distance to the other man with a couple steps.

"What is it?"

There were three sheets printed on cheap paper. Beef Scott fanned them out and then handed them to Ahab who started flipping them back and forth.

"It's an email string between Mathias and someone named Britta Vragi. Looks like Mathias printed it out earlier today and then either forgot to take it or assumed it wasn't important enough to save and the fire would get it."

"Oh, shit," Ahab said, reading. He had finished reading through the email string that covered three pages, and flipped back to the first page again.

"Sven," Ahab said, reading the initial email. "We will prepare Protocol Granite for several team members. Names to follow. They have ventured beyond established parameters and have become expendable. A show of faith payout to the surviving family even though they all have signed ironclad liability waivers. I need you to do a deep dive on family."

"Yeah."

"Jesus," Rick said. "That's pretty cold."

"I didn't recognize any of the names. Looks like some sort of cultural cross-section. Five names and then what I assume are their ID numbers. What do you make of it?"

Ahab shrugged. He put the small sheaf of papers down on the printer tray and turned back around.

"Support is at the gate, sir," came the voice from mission control. The data extraction team had made it onsite. Ahab nodded.

"Roger that," he said and turned back to Beef. "We'll make sure our boys see that. Looks like a group of explorers stumbled onto something they weren't supposed to."

"And they're about to get erased."

CHAPTER ELEVEN
THE BUILDING

THERE WAS a brief pause as the expedition research team stood ready on the platform. One of the technicians quickly reached up and pressed a button on the side of her phone headset. Unconsciously, she dipped her head as she spoke in a quiet register—it was a subtle act of secrecy that Damon noticed from halfway across the room. He could see her lips move, but couldn't hear what she was saying.

"Yes, ma'am," the technician said. She looked down at her clipboard. "Butcher, Lofton, Brunarski, Hollyfeld, Park, and Tolliver. Same team as earlier."

She paused, nodding her head. Damon Butcher wrinkled his forehead. The technician nodded her head one final time.

"Yes, ma'am. Of course. At once. Thank you." She reached up and pressed the button on the side of her headset to disconnect the call. She looked to her right, at another technician and gave him a quick "thumbs up" motion. He nodded in return and hit a quick keystroke on his computer. Suddenly, the countdown clock started at 5, 4…

The technician who had spoken on the phone quietly said to herself, "Good luck."

* *

It wasn't even a heated debate, really. The expedition team had met once again in the awkwardly positioned conference room to discuss the pros and cons of going back to Old Russia, as that time period was known. Finally, Miles joined the meeting and said that they had Britta's blessing. They had a set mission parameter and would explore the road, take samples, and scan as much data as they could. Cadey and Damon shot each other a sideways glance. They had yet to share the information about the hidden building for fear of getting in trouble.

Since they had the go-ahead to go back to the past, they would let the team find the building organically. But, of course, they could guide the group without anyone actually realizing it.

Which is what they did.

And now, they stood in front of the structure.

"What the *fuck*?" Miles asked the environment in general.

It was a stunning sight. The team had walked several hundred meters while taking samples along the road. They had found numerous sections of concrete and even a few samples of a style of metalworking. Everyone was very excited by these discoveries. As they were starting to pack up to return, Cadey Park had looked up and indicated a clump of trees to the left of the road.

"Hey," she said. "What's that?"

And then she started walking. Damon Butcher was the first to follow and then the remaining four members of the expedition. As they rounded the corner, they reached the building.

"Oh, shit," Damon said.

The building stood three stories high and was greatly deteriorated. Parts of it were still intact while sections of it resembled a Roman ruin. One entire wing was completely overgrown with weeds, trees, and brush. Above the huge double-doors at the main entrance was a series of letters that were not immediately recognizable.

"What language is that?" Damon asked the group.

Emi Tolliver, the team's language expert, simply shrugged her shoulders.

"Outside of that one—there—vaguely resembling the number 5," she said. "These characters don't share any characteristics with any language I know. Or even one I've seen."

Damon turned to Miles.

"Did you guys build this? Was this some sort of early experiment? The original time-travel landing pad?"

Miles was quiet for a moment, and then slowly shook his head.

"No," he said. "Not that I know of."

It was stylistic lettering that was clearly the name of the corporation or, at the very least, the name of the building.

"So," Lazlo Hollyfeld said. "This building is 100 million years old."

It was at once a statement and a question. The rest of the team was silent. The background was punctuated by a loud, high-pitched roar. It was an odd wheezing sound that didn't necessarily inspire fear, but the team—minus Damon—immediately turned toward it.

Calvin saw that Damon wasn't eliciting the proper response.

"*T-rex*," Brunarski said. "Sounds like someone's hungry."

"That's not what a tyrannosaur sounds like," Damon said and then caught himself at the end of the statement. Calvin smiled.

"That's not what movies and cartoons *think* a tyrannosaur sounds like," he said. "But this is what they actually sound like. I think you're going to have a lot of these moments. So much of what we think we know about dinosaurs are just guesses. Typically based on bones. Coloring. Hair. Feathers. Scales. Sounds. All guesses. We have the ability to set the record straight."

There were various dinosaur tracks in the area. Only Miles seemed to notice a small section of ground that seemed to be covered in tire tracks.

Damon nodded. The *T-rex* sounded again. Followed by another. The sounds were closer, but still several hundred meters away.

"Maybe we should go inside," Lazlo said. "Take a look around. Let them finish their hunt before we try to walk back."

Miles, at a loss for words, just nodded.

* *

"Son of a bitch," Calvin said.

He had been one of the first through the door and had activated the face-plate-mounted LED flashlights that were attached at his temples. Right now, he was looking down at the floor. He could see beautiful tilework and expert craftsmanship hiding behind a thin layer of dust, dirt, and general grime. There were several spots, however, that were uncovered. There were clearly footprints all up and down this grand hallway.

"Wow," Cadey said.

The six team members formed a semi-circle several meters inside the main entrance. The corridor stretched off into the distance and the section they were currently in was about four meters wide. There were a few doors that lined this area and it ultimately seemed to spill into a larger open room.

"There's been recent activity here," Damon said. "Human activity."

He actually lifted up his boot to look at the sole.

"The tread pattern matches," he said, and then lowered his foot back to the floor.

"What the fuck is going on?" Emi asked the group as a whole.

"Maybe we shouldn't be here," Miles said.

As if on cue, they heard the high-pitched roar of the *T-rex*...that seemed to be joined by two more beasts. Heavy footfalls rattled the walls.

"Let's get a look at the layout of this place," Cadey said. "We can come back properly equipped."

"Agreed," Calvin said.

* *

Outside of the footprints that dominated the corridor, one of the first things the expedition team noticed was the slight variation in size. Everything seemed slightly larger than it should have been. It was almost as if they were operating on a 75 percent scale. The doors seemed too big. The door latches seemed too big. There were one or two benches scattered throughout the walkway—which seemed too big.

"It just feels strange," Damon said. "The proportions are off."

"A super-ancient civilization," Hollyfeld said.

"It's impossible to tell how old this building is, right now, as is," Brunarski said. "Hundreds of years? Thousands? We're already 100 million years into Earth's past. It's possible that a civilization has just gone extinct."

"Right. I mean," Damon said. "How long would it take for the environment to reclaim a building?"

The team continued to walk down the hallway. There were metal letters on the floor—that had, presumably, fallen off the wall—that were similar in style to the characters on the outside of the building. It was becoming obvious that the main corridor would soon empty into a large courtyard.

Cadey shrugged.

"There have been several studies," she said. "Realistically, an entire city could be reclaimed by nature in as little as 500 years. Obviously, it depends on numerous factors."

"Sure." Calvin nodded. "That would be a good earmark. We don't know what this area looked like 500 years ago. Maybe this is a solitary building. Maybe it was in the center of a metropolis."

"100 million plus 500 years old," Lazlo Hollyfeld said, stepping into the courtyard at the end of the corridor. "This is the discovery of a lifetime."

* *

The courtyard of the building was immense. It seemed like a multi-purpose room with a stage on one side, a set of stone bleachers on the other, and numerous structures that defied definition. The room was dominated by a series of sculptures along the north wall. The largest one, nearly filling the space from stone floor to curved ceiling, was a tree that was carved to resemble a woman. Her features were blurred and out of proportion. She looked like the 3D representation of an impressionist's painting. All the right pieces were in all the right places, but the proportions seemed somehow...wrong.

The team stood motionless just inside the courtyard's grand entrance. Twelve different beams of light played all across the oversized room.

Emi pointed to a section of the ceiling.

"There's some sort of nest up there," she said.

"We shouldn't be here," Miles said, as if sensing some sort of danger.

* *

One hundred million years away, Britta Vragi sat behind her enormous desk and watched the attack of the unknown dinosaur again. They had lost several team members during that excursion. She had worked with her counterpart at the storage and operations facility to write up a narrative about their final moments. Luckily, only one of the team members, a man named Harrison, had any family that needed to be notified. Certainly, it had been a factor in hiring throughout her time with Allied Genetics.

There was a knock on the door and it quickly opened.

"Beale," Britta said. "I need you to go out there and bring them back."

He nodded.

"Minimal force," she said. And he nodded again.

"Okay," he said. "I'll bring 'em back."

With that, he turned and left the office. Britta, for her part, turned back to her laptop and started the gruesome footage yet again.

* *

The expedition team had finished exploring the large courtyard and progressed past it. The room broke into a defined V-shape and the two corridors expanded away from the huge room —one path traveling toward the east and one to the west. The team chose to venture down the west path first.

"Is that blood?" Damon asked, pausing near a section of the hallway that seemed to contain a high level of activity. The dust and dirt was disturbed. There seemed to be bullet holes in a section of the wall. Damon had crouched down to center his flashlights on an area of the floor.

He touched the dark brown liquid with the tips of his fingers. It was dry, but still a bit tacky. He held the fingertips up close to his face. The computer imaging system in his faceplate took several pictures and began to analyze. It would be impossible to get a full chemical analysis without a sample, but it certainly behaved like dried blood.

Emi Tolliver bent down and ran a cotton swab across the stain, dropped the swab into a protective vinyl test tube, sealed it, and dropped it into a pocket on the side of her uniform.

"Guys," Cadey said. She had moved past the mess and was staring at a door 12 meters further down the corridor.

Everyone stood and jogged down to meet her.

The doorjamb itself was destroyed. It resembled a gaping wound in the right side of the corridor. Some sort of gate hung loosely, destroyed, away from the door's frame.

"Look at the splinter marks," Cadey said, pointing at a section of the wall. "This gate was holding something in that room that didn't appreciate it."

They paused as a tyrannosaur roar rattled what was left of the skylight above the courtyard. Then, there was another sound they couldn't identify.

"We *really* shouldn't be here," Miles said.

The rest of the team cautiously stepped into the room. Miles and Damon were still in the corridor.

Damon put a hand on Miles's chest, fingers splayed, stopping his momentum.

"What's going on, man?" Damon said. "What do you know about this place?"

"What are you talking about?"

"You fought hard to not bring us back here, then you caved," he said. "Now, you've mentioned a half-dozen times that we shouldn't be here. You know more than you're letting on."

Miles glared at his friend and slowly reached up and removed Damon's hand from his chest.

"We are in a hostile environment, 100 million years in the past. We are hopelessly underequipped with what sounds like a family of tyrannosaurs stalking prey a football field away from us. Yes. I think we should head back. Come back with a security force or something."

Damon paused, looked at his friend.

"What kind of security force?"

Miles didn't have a chance to answer as there was a voice from down the hallway.

"Exit the room, now."

It was Beale, weapon raised, flanked by two other O221 soldiers on either side of him. They all had weapons drawn and were slowly advancing down the hallway.

"Mr. Lofton," Beale said. "If you don't mind."

The full expedition team had exited the destroyed room and now stood in the wide corridor facing the assault force.

"What's going on?" Emi asked the group in general. "Who are these guys?"

"Objekt 221, Allied Genetics, employs a private military force," Miles said. "It appears that we've overstepped our boundaries."

"Mr. Lofton," Beale said again.

Miles nodded and turned away from his researchers. He walked down the corridor and stood behind the five soldiers. Beale and his force remained in formation, standing opposite the five members of the expedition team.

There was a high-pitched roar from outside. Closer. Followed by two others. There seemed to be three distinct *T-rex* adults somewhere outside. No one inside Building 5 flinched.

"So, you're just going to leave us here?" Calvin asked. "We're employees of this company, too, you know?"

Silence from Beale. It seemed like he was considering his options.

"Nope," he finally said. "We're all going back together. We wanted to contain the situation on this side before you caused any irreparable harm."

Through this, Miles remained silent. He was scowling, but at no person in specific. For his part, Damon was glaring at his friend.

"Let's go," Beale said and gestured with his black shotgun. The other four men, carrying submachine guns, stepped to the side to allow the five scientists to pass. They didn't, however, lower their weapons.

* *

They walked back down the west corridor to the courtyard in a caravan. Beale and Miles were in the lead. The five researchers came next, flanked by two soldiers, and followed by two more. They walked slowly, steadily, with a purpose. They traveled back through the courtyard into the main stem of the capital Y-layout of Building 5.

In the distance, Damon could see the main entrance and the dense foliage beyond it. Just outside the large doors were parked two vehicles. They looked like cross-over SUVs, with significant additions. Huge, run-flat tires. Flood lights. Metal bars across all the windows. Painted a deep green. They looked like up-armored military vehicles.

Suddenly, there was a cacophony of screeches and squeals followed by thunderous footfalls. Beale raised his right hand, making a fist, signaling to the team to stop. With a huge crash, a group of *Triceratops* ran past, knocking into one of the vehicles and smashing it into the other. Mere seconds behind them were the three tyrannosaurs, chasing their dinner. The two vehicles, unfortunately, were trampled.

As the footfalls faded off into the distance, the group stood motionless five meters into the facility. They could smell gasoline and various other chemicals leaking from the ruined military trucks. Even at this distance, it was an overpowering scent.

"Ah, shit," Beale said. He turned slightly and smiled over his shoulder. "I hope you wore your comfy shoes."

CHAPTER TWELVE
THE RETURN

BRITTA WAS no stranger to difficult managerial decisions. Early in her career, she had found it necessary to terminate an entire wing of employees. She left only the department head. Everyone else was escorted out of the building by armed security personnel. Not only was it the week before Christmas, but it was the week before a crucial experiment was due to generate the critical output. Rather than waiting to remove these workers—it was a loss prevention issue—after the research had run its course, she decided it was more important to cut this particular tumor out of the building at once.

The division struggled, but they reloaded and completed their work admirably.

She was, right now, having lunch with Objekt 221's head of personnel—Marcus Osborne —in the executive cafeteria.

"Yes," she said, driving a forkful of peas around her plate. "I discussed the situation with Mathias earlier today."

"Okay, good," Marcus said. He hadn't touched his meal and knew he'd be snacking all day. They'd never faced an event of this magnitude before, and he was more than a little troubled. "Can I ask you something?"

Britta nodded.

"Why did I allow them to go back without simply containing the situation here?"

Marcus nodded in response.

"Yeah." He dabbed the corners of his mouth with his napkin, removing food that had never been there in the first place.

"That's a fair question," she said, giving up and putting her fork down next to the plate. "And a good one. I'm not entirely sure. I weighed the options and felt we could control the situation better grabbing them on the other side, bringing them back, and putting them in isolation, rather than marching them through the facility in front of everyone."

Marcus was quiet for a moment. Pensive.

"There's a maintenance tunnel leading directly from the transport pad to Room 4," he said.

"Uh huh," Britta said. "We can get them through without anyone even knowing."

Again, Marcus went silent.

"Wouldn't it have been...?" He leaned in closer, lowering his voice. "Wouldn't it have been easier to have them encounter an *accident* on the other side?"

"An accident of that magnitude? Our insurance rates would skyrocket." Britta smiled. "There's no right answer. Maybe I wanted to see if they'd uncover something we missed. Maybe I gave it a few hours to see if they'd get any more footage of our Unclassified. Honestly, I'm not sure."

"I suppose that's honest," Marcus said. "What did Mathias say?"

Britta shrugged.

"We emailed back and forth to plan the logistics and then he went quiet," she said, fully giving up on her lunch plate. The waiter came past and cleared their table. Another man poured them each a cup of coffee. "I suppose I should check on that. I got the call that Lofton's expedition team went back right after. I guess I got a bit distracted."

Marcus nodded and dabbed the corners of his mouth again. Again, for no reason.

"It's easy to do," he said. "Beale's back there?"

Britta nodded.

"Yep," she said. "I expect him back any minute now."

"Okay," Marcus said, standing up. He ran his hands down the pleats on the front of his slacks. "Call me if you need me there."

"Of course," Britta said, and sipped her coffee.

* *

Leaving the trampled remains of their two transport vehicles stomped into the ancient Earth near the entrance of Building 5, Beale and his prisoners began the long march toward the Anvil Canyon base. They had just more than a mile to travel over relatively flat terrain. Unfortunately, they were beginning to lose the light and predators were starting to swarm the area.

Beale was under orders to not harm the five members of the expedition team, but the five researchers were under no illusions about what they would likely face when they got back to Allied Genetics. Likely, there would be some sort of discipline—possibly termination.

The worst part would be overcoming the stigma attached to being fired from a high-security organization. It might make it difficult to get another job.

Damon, however, was crestfallen. He had known Miles for years and felt betrayed at the lack of communication. Even when Damon put the question directly to him—what do you know? —Miles had held fast to the lie.

More than that, however, Damon was certain that this experience was going to end much worse than being fired. *Termination*, he thought, *in a very literal sense*.

"Keep it moving," Beale said without turning back to the line of prisoners behind him. "We'll have some pretty bright starlight, but when the sun goes down, we hit full dark pretty quickly. You can go night vision, but no flashlights."

They marched on in silence, keeping close to the tree-line, away from the dilapidated remains of the road. They were in the same formation as earlier with Beale and Miles in the lead, followed by the five researchers. They were flanked by two soldiers with the final two soldiers bringing up the rear. It was a mystery to the five team members as to why one of the soldiers had given Miles a sidearm.

Everyone on the expedition team was quiet, contemplating what was going on, processing it in their own way. Finally, it was Calvin who spoke up. Cadey Park was walking next to him, but he could have been talking to anyone in hushed tones.

"I'm having trouble coming to grips with what's going on," he said, looking forward.

"Being led by gun-toting thugs, death-march style, to face our boss?" Cadey responded under her breath, but loud enough for Calvin to hear speaking off mic—as well as the soldier immediately to her right.

Calvin shook his head.

"I mean us stumbling into evidence of a super-ancient civilization," he said. "It took me a while to get used to the idea of documenting, studying, and analyzing plants and animals from 100 million years ago. But," he paused, "what did we just see?"

They walked in silence.

Damon, directly behind the two of them could hear the conversation, but chose not to add anything yet.

"I mean," Calvin continued, staring straight ahead, raising his hands a bit, palms-up, "it seems obvious that this planet could create life twice or even three times in its six billion year history. And, given generally the same circumstances, environment, and challenges—these different civilizations might advance in similar fashions. But did we just see clear evidence that we aren't the first humans to live on this planet?"

Cadey was nodding.

"I think so, Cal," she said. "I'm trying to think of a scenario where this building might represent something else. We are time travelers, by the very definition of our job description. Who's to say that Building 5 isn't an earlier attempt by O221 to build a base on this end of the time jump?"

They walked a bit more in silence.

"Best guess?" she said, folding her arms across her chest. "There was a civilization of proto-humans living on planet Earth 100 million years ago. By the time we rose to power, all traces of their existence has been wiped out."

"That's enough," Beale said. His voice came in loud and clear over the faceplate speakers. "And turn your internal mics back on. I don't want any external sound if we can help it. Many things out here want to kill us. I want to stay off their radar."

They walked in silence as the sun continued to set on ancient Crimea. Emi finally spoke up at the end of the formation.

"What's waiting for us in O221, Beale?" she asked. "Termination? Thumbscrews? Waterboarding?"

No one spoke for several steps.

"I'm sure there'll be some sort of discipline," he said. "But it can't be as bad as being eaten by a dinosaur."

He meant this as half joke, half warning, but as if on cue, the underbrush exploded in front of them. Fifty meters past the team, a dinosaur erupted out of the trees and paused momentarily in the clearing caused by the remains of the road. The team stopped as one, walking on the fringe of the foliage cover. Everyone's HUD lit up simultaneously. The image of the dinosaur in front of them was highlighted red with the flashing text DANGER immediately next to it. The note UC-0104 hovered ominously above the dinosaur.

"Oh, fuck," Beale said under his breath, but fully audible to the soldiers and scientists in tow.

They were looking at an uncategorized apex predator. The word "UNCLASSIFIED" was blinking on their screens with numbers and data flashing all around the image perimeter. Soon, the word was replaced by the text UC-0104 as the shared computer accessed the saved data—comparing the image to the stored database.

In the fading light, it was difficult to see the coloring of the creature. The team could barely make out the deep green—almost brown—hide, lined with spines, and ringed with deep blue coloring. Twin rows of spikes ran the length of its back and tapered as they traveled down the tail. Most striking, though, was that the dinosaur stood atop two thick, muscular legs and had four arms erupting from its trunk. This was an apex predator standing more than 10 feet tall.

Staring straight at them.

UC-0104 snarled.

Beale's voice came over their faceplate speakers, urgent yet quiet.

"We. Need. To. Start. Moving," he said. "Into the trees. Slowly. Now."

The soldiers, on Beale's order, started slowly walking to the side. The temptation to drop to the ground and crab walk was strong, but, instead, they all simply walked sideways, grape-vine style, to reach the cover provided by the heavy foliage. For the most part, the researchers followed suit. Emi Tolliver and Lazlo Hollyfeld, however, were frozen to the ground, mouths agape, staring at a type of dinosaur they had never seen. The motion had attracted UC's attention. He continued to snarl and, now, took a few cautious steps toward the group.

"Let's go," Beale said, noticing that his rear flank was bunching up. "Jackson. Look out."

"Sir," the soldier on the left flank said, keeping his eyes on UC. "It's advancing."

"I see," Beale said. "We'll kill it if we have to. We'll be back tomorrow to capture it anyway."

"Capture?" Calvin said, stepping to his right.

There were a few moments of tense silence until Miles spoke up.

"Allied Genetics is not only recording what happens over here, but capturing specimens that might prove useful. Genetically. There is no fossil record of UC-0104 and he is now in our capture protocol to carefully analyze his destructive power." He paused. Beale had stopped moving. He was looking at the researcher, mouth open.

"Dude," he said.

"We have special equipment that we use to capture and transport the specimens." Miles shrugged. "I'm sure Beale only brought people-based equipment, though."

Jackson, in the back of the group, had taken his eyes off the team and looked at UC. In doing so, his feet got caught up with Lazlo's. Both men grunted and fell to the ground. The action pushed Emi out of the way, into the actual forest.

Everyone was nearly in the forest. The second soldier in the rear stooped to help Jackson and Lazlo to their feet. He kept his weapon pointed at UC-0104 the entire time.

"Tuoy," Beale said, turning his head left and speaking to the soldier on the extreme left flank. "Smoke."

"Copy that," Tuoy said. He reached his right hand around to his lower back and removed two golf ball-sized silver spheres from the combat webbing there. "Two out," he said, lobbing the two metal balls in the direction of the continuously, but cautiously, advancing UC. They arced through the air and landed about five meters apart, five meters in front of the dinosaur. There was a small thump as the two spheres exploded and covered the area in a gaseous cloud.

"That'll slow him down, but won't stop him," Beale said. "Move it."

* *

All 11 people were in the forest. They heard UC roar twice while he was trying to find his way out of the chemical fog, but that was it. They couldn't hear anything moving through the trees behind them. Suddenly, they heard the high-pitched roar of one of the tyrannosaurs.

"Oh, for fuck's sake," Beale said.

The entire team stopped and were sweeping their gazes and weaponry back and forth searching for the source of the sound. They had all switched to night vision mode on their faceplates. It was full dark.

"Okay, let's—" Beale started and was cut off. From their right, UC-0104 blasted out of a clump of trees while everyone was distracted. The dinosaur lifted Jackson off his feet with two powerful arms and continued to run away—never slowing down. He hit Hollyfeld across the face and chest with the spike-laden tail. Hollyfeld went down. As sudden

94

as he had appeared, UC was gone. They heard Jackson scream once and then was silenced.

Hollyfeld was writhing on the ground, ribs cracked. His faceplate was starred with a shatter mark, but had not caved in.

"Weapons free," Beale said. "Tango live. Light 'em up."

* *

"Good God," Britta said.

She was sitting in a corner of her office. There was a bank of 20 small flatscreen monitors attached to the wall. Britta leaned forward in her red leather chair. These monitors represented the only live feed link between Objekt 221 and the mirror base in ancient Crimea. *The Other Side*, as they liked to call it.

There was no video feed, but, through quantum foam—a spectacularly long explanation that she never attempted to nail down—they could receive the transmission of each expedition team member's vital statistics along a certain wavelength. Each of the monitors contained a name at the top and several graphs and numeric readouts that painted the picture of health. There was an algorithm that analyzed the metric data and condensed it into a text box in the bottom right corner. *Elevated heartrate and ascending perspiration levels indicate anxiety approaching fear*, for example.

She could see Miles and his five researchers lined up as well as Beale and his four soldiers. One of the monitors worried her. One of the monitors elicited her verbal outburst.

Deceased, the text read along the bottom corner of Jackson's monitor.

Broken ribs, bruised lungs, catastrophic failure of protective faceplate eminent, the text read along the bottom corner of Hollyfeld's monitor.

"What the fuck happened?" she asked herself. "Those faceplates are supposed to be unbreakable."

She rolled the chair across the tile floor back to the corner of her enormous desk. She reached for the phone. *Why the hell was Owl Mountain not answering?*

* *

The four remaining soldiers plus Miles formed a star around the five researchers—with Lazlo Hollyfeld lying on the ground in the center of the formation. The soldiers were scanning the area with the night vision filter on their faceplates.

Lazlo coughed and blood splattered the inside of his mask. Emi had her hand across his chest, fingers splayed. She could feel his labored breathing—as well as hear it over her speakers. His eyes were closed, drooling blood. It was darker—it seemed to Damon that it was darker than it should be. Emi looked up to Calvin and shook her head softly.

He coughed again and went still.

"Shit," Beale said, seeing the warning on his faceplate. Lazlo had died of internal injuries. "We have to move."

"Do we bring him with us?" Miles asked.

Beale thought for a moment.

"We bring him," he said. "McCann."

A soldier named McCann bent to lift Hollyfeld's lifeless body up off the ground. Lazlo was tall and thin and weighed about 160 pounds. The soldier balanced him over his right shoulder, holding his submachine gun in his left.

"No shame in calling it out when it's time to trade," Beale said not only to McCann, but to the other soldiers to make sure his point rang true. "We have a mile. Let's rock and roll."

* *

The team made it only 50 meters deeper into the forest under cover of darkness before everything went haywire. With the proximity warning flashing on their HUDs, the team didn't know whether to run for the building or try to hide. They were getting no indications from their thermal vision, but night vision outlined three fast-moving theropods. They were still nearly a mile away from the HQ building.

"Defensive formation," Beale called over the team chat.

Immediately, the four remaining soldiers formed the points of a compass around the four researchers. McCann dropped Hollyfeld's corpse a few meters away near a heavy clump of bushes. He took up position as the east point. Miles, drawing his sidearm, joined him.

The proximity alarm was replaced by a wire-frame outline of the three dinosaurs. They were *Deinonychus*—popularized incorrectly by the Jurassic Park movie—and generally recognized in popular media as

Velociraptors. Walking on two legs, with heavily muscled arms and a long tail, the *Deinonychus* stretched more than 15 feet long and were known for having a huge claw in the center of each foot. In fact, the name is Greek for "terrible claw." While the team couldn't see the three predators, the HUD database described them as dark brown with yellow cabalistic markings.

The three predators arrived at the small clearing at the same time. They formed a triangle around the group of humans and stayed just out of effective weapon range. A crash in the underbrush pulled everyone's attention to the west. After three long seconds, they turned back to their natural positions. The body of Lazlo Hollyfeld was gone.

"Fuck," McCann said.

"What is it?" Miles asked, sweat dripping into his right eye. He squeezed it shut to protect it from the stinging, salty liquid.

Before McCann could answer, a new sound dominated the landscape. It was the low-pitched growl of the 0104. UC had finally caught back up with the group after the earlier encounter. It shook off the effects of the chemical cloud.

Sensing that the larger predator would steal their kill, the three *Deinonychus* attacked with a speed and ferocity that the humans did not expect. They rushed at the huge dinosaur who simply crouched into a defensive pose and bared his enormous teeth. He bunched the hands at the ends of his two upper arms into fists and the two lower hands were opened wide—claws pointed at the onrushing group.

The first attacker leapt into the air, right leg outstretched. He reared back, tensing his muscles to eviscerate the UC with the terrible claw. In what must have looked like a quick flinch, the UC caught the huge dinosaur with his upper arms and raked both lower arms, claws extended, across the leaping *Deinonychus* torso. Mortally wounded, it let out a high-pitched yelp as blood and intestines rained down around its feet.

Already on the move, the second *Deinonychus* howled in anguish as it saw its fallen partner. Without slowing down its charge, it splayed its claws wide and rushed directly at the UC. For its part, the UC simply dropped the dead body directly into the onrushing dino's path, causing it to stumble.

The UC reared back and kicked the second *Deinonychus* squarely in the chest. It went down in a heap.

The third *Deinonychus*, sensing the turning tide of the battle, immediately stopped its attack and scampered off into the forest. The UC roared and gave chase.

The mission team stood in silence for a moment, watching the area where the two dinosaurs disappeared deeper into the ancient Crimean forest.

"I thought the *Deinonychus* was exclusive to North America," Emi said, breaking the team's stunned silence.

Suddenly, the dinosaur who had been kicked in the chest grunted, rolled over, and attempted to regain his balance and stand up.

"Fuck," Miles said.

Before the word had completely escaped his mouth, the downed dinosaur was up and rushed at Derekson, the soldier at the south point of the compass, and Calvin Brunarski, who stood immediately to the soldier's left. With a full roundhouse kick—giant foot-claw extended— the dinosaur tore through the torsos of both men. They fell to the ground in a puddle of their own blood, dead before their legs had even given out.

The remaining three soldiers opened fire with small arms and riddled the body of the *Deinonychus* with bullet holes. Miles panicked and fired his borrowed sidearm. Unfortunately, his first two shots sailed wide and he hit Emi Tolliver squarely in the back. She died instantly and crumpled in a heap next to Calvin.

* *

Britta, watching one monitor after another go dark, was screaming at the office wall.

"Get back here," she yelled.

* *

"Leave 'em," Beale shouted, reloading his weapon.

The team had been cut in half. Beale and his two soldiers Miller and McCann were only guarding two researchers—Damon Butcher and Cadey Park. Miles, of course, was aligned with the soldiers. The team turned as one and started running back in the direction of the facility. They had made it nearly a quarter mile when the UC returned to the small clearing. He was carrying the *Deinonychus* head as a trophy and had blood dripping from his massive jaws down his torso. He looked around the carnage in front of him and didn't bother chasing after the remaining prey.

CHAPTER THIRTEEN
THE FINAL DEBRIEFING

SERGOTT SOLUTIONS wore its distinction as an American company lightly. They had five offices worldwide that were each staffed with a generous mixture of diverse talents. Three of the five were in the United States—San Francisco, Chicago, Miami—with the fourth and fifth being in London and Beijing. Clay Reed was the operational leader of the London office. He sat in a small conference room at a circular table, joined by the four heads of the various military teams operating throughout Europe.

Reed had passed a set of white binders, each three inches thick, to the four men seated around the table. They were all Wraith field commanders currently stationed in Europe. Alex Scott, Rick Everson, Jon Culver, and Eric Bilkins. They were all roughly the same age and experience level. In silence, they all started flipping through the binders, heavy with printed reports. They knew they'd have a few minutes of silence before Reed started in on the presentation.

No one broke protocol even though all four men were making notes, highlighting phrases and scratching out thoughts on legal pads throughout the silence.

The actual names of each installation?

Eradicated scientists?

Gene manipulation?

A robotic octopus?

Clay Reed leaned forward and pulled open his own binder. He had gone over it several times in the hour since his staff had collated the data. His paperwork was stuffed with sticky-notes, highlights, and a printed speech that he was about to give full of notes for the military wing.

He cleared his throat and the men all looked up from their binders to the boss.

"This is a summary with relevant information cobbled together from the three gigs versus Allied Genetics," he started. It was a prepared opening, similar to dozens of like briefings he had given in the past. "The majority of the data comes from the most recent excursion—Owl Mountain. Known in internal documents as *Rainier Mesa*. Turns out that facility was designed for data storage. They had destroyed the vast majority of their stored data, but the office of Sven Mathias was untouched and yielded a good deal of information."

He paused, not for dramatic effect, but to look down at his prepared statement. Reed knew he had to build to the final big message, but there was so much information here that it was easy to get lost.

"There're a few pages in here talking specifically about the history of Allied Genetics and Precision Robotics—our client on this series of missions. The latter has paid a healthy sum for our particular brand of industrial sabotage and data mining. Nothing in our initial research suggests any overlapping business areas, but Precision's motivations are their own. We can get into some of that a bit later. And, of course, read the binder thoroughly to familiarize yourself with the final mission for the client."

He cleared his throat, slid the binder slightly to his right, opened to a page, and continued reading from his notes.

"We're going to start, basically, from the back first. The Owl Mountain mission." He turned to nod at Alex and Rick in turn. "Nice work, gentlemen." The two men nodded in response. "When this data was presented to Precision Robotics, they immediately ponied up the funds for a fourth mission. In short, it was the forgotten email that grabbed their interest. Protocol Granite. Clearly, a group of researchers on Allied's payroll stumbled into something they weren't supposed to. They are scheduled for termination."

He looked at his notes.

"Britta Vragi, the chief of Allied's facility in Crimea—known internally as Anvil Canyon—had instructed Sven to begin preparing the necessary documentation and start researching any surviving family members that would need paying off. Precision does not want this to happen. Since we're behind the eight ball on this one, time is of the essence."

Something had caught the attention of Alex Scott, call sign Beef. He flipped through the four main chapters of his binder while Reed was finishing his thought. Beef made some notes on his legal pad and Reed stopped talking.

"What is it, Scott?"

"Not sure, sir," he said. "I'm not sure there's a deeper meaning. Maybe just some innocuous wordplay."

"Go on," Reed said.

"The names of these facilities. Rainier Mesa. Anvil Canyon. The island off Florida is referred to as Frenchman's Flat. These are all…"

"The names of former nuclear test sites."

"Yes," Alex said. "Of course, they must be named in honor of. Anvil Hill, which is, I suppose, where the reference to Anvil Canyon originated, was actually in Australia."

"Frenchman Flat—a slight variation of the name—was in Nevada," Jon "Beans" Culver offered.

"We picked up on that," Reed said. "We're not sure if there's any actual association with the various facilities. We're considering putting some IT people on it to see if the trend continues. We know of at least three other Allied facilities worldwide. Best we can tell, they're just trying to be clever. Allied is into a lot of stuff, but none of it looks energy-related."

Reed turned to the second page of his prepared notes and flipped forward through his binder. He was silent and the four men all sat waiting for him to continue.

"The scientists are important," he finally continued. "But they are not the most shocking part of this story." He waited for a moment. He had given a thousand mission briefings in his lifetime, but none as strange as this one.

"Allied Genetics has developed a time portal to send their researchers back to the dinosaur era." The four men jerked in shock, their chairs sliding across the polished concrete floor. They all reached for their binders in unison. "They have devoted an entire facility to coming up with new and exciting human-dinosaur cross-modifications. Hochhaus, the flak tower, is the hub for this operation. We interrupted their experiments, however, as their specimen was still being tested and housed at the Port Radnovich facility."

"Frenchman's Flat," Beef suggested.

Clay nodded in response.

"According to internal documents, this project started nearly a year ago. They've been doing extensive planning and experimentation. The first viable specimen was in holding at Frenchman's Flat. Their timing was just unlucky."

"I'd say," Everson said under his breath.

"In any event," Reed continued, "you'll see the high-level summary in your binders. This is all considered mission prep. You'll be going to the belly of the beast. Alpha Complex. Anvil Canyon. Objekt 221."

The men, the four field commanders, started flipping to various pages of the mission binder. They were all going to different parts of the document, making various notes. Clay Reed reached across his body to a small stack of paperwork on his right. He picked up four manila folders and started sliding them around the table.

"Sir, mission parameters?" Beans Culver asked.

"Affirmative, soldier." Reed sat back into his chair and leaned forward. He pulled his version of the mission parameters—the folders he had just slid to his men—from the inside pocket of his binder. "We'll go through this step by step. Scott and Everson will be boots on the ground. Culver will run overwatch from the remote. Bilkins will bat cleanup."

"Like always." Eric "Sixpack" Bilkins grinned at Alex, who nodded back to him in response.

"You wish, buddy." Alex smiled.

Beans Culver ignored the friendly banter as he started flipping through the mission parameters. It was a fairly short report that listed suggested weaponry, vehicles, ingress, and egress. There was a print of the last-known blueprint of the facility with some notes added by various contractors who were questioned. There was a timing schedule and profiles of the five scientists mentioned by name in the email exchange between Britta and Sven. There was one page that Beans was reading through a second time.

"I see that we're starting with a gag," he said, still looking down at his folder, not addressing anyone in particular.

"Yes, Jon," said Reed. "Yes, we are."

CHAPTER FOURTEEN
THE BACK OF THE BUILDING

IT WASN'T much longer until the survivors reached the Gamma Complex. Both the security team and the team of researchers were in tatters. They had sprinted the final half-mile through the trees, listening to the various hoots and howls of the different predators in the area. On the edge of terror and exertion, their faceplate HUDs were displaying various warnings—both in proximity alerts and in physical danger.

Damon's lungs were scalding and he could feel his heart thundering in his ears.

"Gamma Complex," Miles said as they slowed to a stop outside a huge steel door. The building was the mirror image of how the research team entered ancient Crimea earlier in the day. In fact, it was simply on the other side of the building, protected by heavy foliage and dense boulders.

They noticed that the building and surrounding clearing was bathed in a gentle blue light. Miles noticed them looking.

"It's UVC lighting," he continued. "Short-wavelength radiation that's generally blocked by the ozone layer. Good for killing germs. Bad for cold-blooded reptiles who are, right now, burning up their stored warmth and energy. They tend to avoid the building at night."

Cadey was breathing heavily, but remained in control. She was craning her neck, looking around the rocks to the corner of the building.

"The two buildings are connected?" she asked the team in general. Beale was punching his code into a panel on the left of the heavy door. He ignored her. "What is this?"

"It's the other side of Gamma Complex," Miles finally answered. "Basically, a mirror image of the mirror image. One side for one type of excursion, one side for another type. There's actually a garage with up-armored vehicles right there."

"Oh," Cadey said. None of the researchers had even commented on the military vehicles that were trampled outside of Building 5. It would make sense that they didn't bring them along from Anvil Canyon.

With an audible *beep* and the heavy thunk of the huge locks disengaging, the door started to swing open.

The blended team rushed through the door as it was opening. Beale waited to go in last, watching the clearing, listening for any approaching danger. Miles went in second to last and Beale heard the breathy growl of the UC breaking into the clearing. The reptile cringed at the blue UVC light, but kept coming. Beale jumped into the airlock and pulled the giant door closed just in time.

"Holy fuck," he said, under his breath, but it still broadcast over the team's comm channel. "Gonna enjoy putting *that* bitch in a cage."

* *

The two sides of the building—military and research—were structurally identical, but differed in details. Where the research side had racks of binders, computers, and clipboards full of tasks, the military side had storage cabinets full of weaponry, protective gear, and keys to transport vehicles. Functionally, they were both modeled after the same area at O221.

Beale and his team hustled the two researchers through the door, into the airlock. They could hear the unclassified predator pounding against the outer door for the entirety of their UVC light and steam bath that served to remove any germs or unwanted pollutants. *Like something that will eventually grow into a giant centipede*, thought Damon as the final thump from outside vibrated the door.

"I think he's had enough of the ultraviolet light," mused Miles. For her part, Cadey just glared at him in response.

The automated countdown ended and the inner door opened. The two soldiers, plus Beale, led Damon and Cadey across the floor to stand in the octagonal launching pad that was surrounded by the steel pillars designed to generate the time-bending graviton field. This huge room was a carbon copy of the mission control room in Anvil Canyon, as well as the one on the other side of this building. Damon turned to look at one of the enormous concrete walls…the wall, he assumed by position, separated the two halves of Gamma Complex. He turned back to the wall of windows that stood opposite. Just like on the other side of the wall, they were given a view of the Cretaceous vista. It was dark, however, and the windows shared certain characteristics with their faceplate HUDs. They were bathed in a green glow—night vision—with several digital readouts on a constant loop. There wasn't a lot going on outside as the cold-blooded predators had by now used up any stored energy from the day and sought their safe-havens.

The screen highlighted what looked like a family of rodents emerging from tunnels and climbing a tree. They started jumping from branch to branch. *Rugosodon eurasiaticus* rolled across the screen as the huge windows began numbering and tracking the beaver-sized rodents.

Damon turned away from the bank of windows and looked at Cadey.

"I'm sorry," he said.

She simply looked down at her feet as the launching pad started to power up.

* *

By the time they arrived back in present-day, there was only one computer specialist in the operations room. In contrast, there were four members of the medical team and four additional security team members.

And Britta Vragi.

The two remaining researchers were whisked away to a confinement room—as Britta had planned—through the hidden corridors in the facility. The two members of Beale's security force took the rest of the day off as the medical staff quickly examined Damon and Cadey. Beale and Britta watched this interaction carefully. The four members of the medical staff finished their examination and left the room.

The mysterious Room 4 looked like a conference room—if you didn't look too closely. There was a table, but it was bolted to the floor. There were HVAC vents, but they were sized for residential rather than commercial. There was a door, but it locked from the outside, both with physical security and an electronic keypad. There was no way to alter the temperature, lighting, or even audio settings from inside the room. One entire wall was glass, but not. It was highly tempered, bulletproof, and shatterproof acrylic. The same material that was used for the company's unbreakable faceplates.

Cadey and Damon both sat on the table's surface, looking out through the window. Britta and Beale stood in the narrow hallway, looking back.

"I've not met you personally, but I'm Britta Vragi," she said. "I'm the operational director of Objekt 221. I'm one of the 12 field vice presidents of Allied Genetics."

Her voice was coming over loud and clear on Room 4's overhead speakers. Both researchers were silent.

"You've presented me with a problem that I'm not sure how to resolve," she continued, and, then, was silent for a moment. "That's not entirely true. I know several ways to resolve it, but I'm not sure which strategy is the best. I could have left you on the other side to die. I could have had you killed there and simply left your bodies to decompose. I can have you killed right now. I can send you to a remote facility, locked away from the world, to do data mining until your heads explode. I can bury you in a Siberian prison."

No one spoke for a moment.

"I'm not sure which path is best," she said. "You will see me as evil, but I'm truly trying to find a compromise that works. You broke the rules. Went off the reservation. Found something that we've kept hidden away for a year."

She stepped forward, toward the glass wall.

"You see, all of the work we're doing is planet-changing. From the time travel, to the observation of live dinosaurs, to the evidence of a super-ancient civilization. Taken individually, any of the three could simply break someone's mind. Factor in all three simultaneously—plus the groundbreaking work we've done in genetics—and no one will know how to react."

She clasped her hands behind her back. It was a relaxed, at-ease position and she furrowed her brow to complete the look.

"We have a very specific timeline to follow to roll-out these various events. And I can't have you fucking up my calendar. So," she continued after taking a deep breath. "What am I to do?"

Neither researcher spoke. Beale, also, remained silent.

After a few moments, Britta shrugged her shoulders. She reached forward and flipped a toggle switch on the control panel that sat below the lock's keypad. This shut off the audio feed into the room.

"Fine," she said to Beale, before turning and walking away—the sound of her heels against the white tile echoed around the small corridor. Beale followed her. It was only when they were out of sight that Cadey turned to Damon.

"How is it that only the *sound* of a person's voice can give you a headache?" she said, and smiled.

* *

Nearly an hour later, Britta sat in her office, flanked by numerous trusted officials from the Anvil Canyon facility. Objekt 221 was the crown jewel of the organization—not only for the obvious operational benefits of the location, but the size of the building itself. As such, Allied Genetics had staffed O221 with the absolute best of the best.

Britta Vragi, Marcus Osborne, Carter Wittington, Jason Beale, Miles Lofton. They sat around the steel table in the corner of Britta's office.

"I wasn't lying," Britta said, speaking to Beale without addressing him. "I'm not entirely sure what to do."

"It was a disaster and a failed containment when we first encountered UC-0104," he said. "This time, we lost three researchers and two of my men. My guy's putting together a plan to capture this thing. Regardless, we're going to have to go back. If you want to dump 'em, we'll dump 'em."

Britta and Carter nodded. Marcus was nonplussed and made a note in his thick, leather-bound day planner. Lofton was silent, but his mouth was agape.

"What are you saying?" Miles finally said. "We're going to kill them? Cadey and Damon? Because they found the building? The road? This is ridiculous."

"We have rules, Miles," Marcus said. "In an effort to keep our business properly segmented, we need to parse out intelligence. Building 5 and the surrounding area were classified. We took great pains to block it out of the technology until such a time when it was deemed appropriate to share with the group as a whole."

"We must protect our investment," Carter chimed in. "If any information gets out, it could ruin our operation. Not only here, but in facilities across the planet. Even now, we are under siege by a paramilitary force. This adds a level of confusion that could wreck the positive strides we've already made."

There was a moment of silence. Britta was thoughtfully making notes on her legal pad. Finally, Miles looked at her across the table.

"So, we're now in the business of eliminating employees? Researchers that were trained—hand-picked—to do a job?"

"*Now*?" Beale grinned and threw strange emphasis on a word Miles had included in his question.

Carter smiled and looked down at his own notepad.

"Look," Marcus said. "You are a talented investigator, Miles, and a brilliant scientist. So, the cutthroat nature of the business shouldn't come as too much of a surprise. Fortunes are gained and lost over a mistimed press release. Careers are broken over a heated email exchange. It is not uncommon for people to be taken out back and roughed up. It is less common, but not a *never* occurrence, that someone has lost their life. To protect a multi-billion dollar organization."

"If you drive like an asshole in Los Angeles, you're likely to get killed for far less," Beale offered.

"This is ridiculous," Miles said again, standing. "I can't believe you're all being so cavalier about this. We're discussing the termination of an employee—in the most literal sense possible. I can't be a part of this."

He stood up from the table and left the meeting.

The four people left at the table sat in silence for a handful of seconds. They shared glances. Marcus looked up from his notes.

"He's one of our best. Possibly the singular best."

"He lacks manners," Carter said.

Britta nodded.

"Perhaps he needs a year of data entry at the Mountain to regain some perspective," Marcus said.

Britta, still silent, nodded at Beale.

Beale stood and left the room.

* *

Cadey and Damon had moved to the far corner of the heavily reinforced conference room. They sat in a corner that was opposite both the glass wall and the locked door. There was nothing in the conference room save for the large table and the eight industrial-grade chairs. There were no guards stationed at the door, but they knew they were not able to escape. They were, unfortunately, at the mercy of Britta Vragi and her decision.

"This sucks," Damon said.

"That might be the understatement of the century," Cadey said.

They sat on the floor. Damon with his legs splayed out. Cadey with her feet flat on the floor. She was hugging the tops of her knees, chin resting on her arms. Damon shrugged.

"Have you guys had anything like this before?" he asked.

Cadey was silent for a moment and then shook her head.

"No," she said. "No. I don't think so. I've heard about a couple people who have died in the last few years. Couple heart attacks. One guy committed suicide. Nothing too crazy, I suppose."

Damon grunted.

"Yeah," he said. "I suppose we've had the same thing at Precision. One guy died in a car accident a couple years ago. I think a lady had cancer."

They were silent for a few breaths.

"Fuck," Cadey said after a moment. She shrugged. "I don't know what's going to happen." She paused. "I'm not sure I want to find out."

She lifted her head and looked around the room for the tenth time during their captivity. Damon shook his head.

"The only weakness I see, possibly, is the electrical panel," he said. "If we could take it off using tools we don't have and short out the mechanism using tools we don't have, we might be able to disengage the lock."

Cadey nodded.

"The electronic lock," she said. "But not the physical lock."

"Yeah," he replied. "Damn."

"Maybe they'll just fire us," she said, putting her head back down on her crossed arms. "I hear Precision is hiring."

* *

Miles Lofton walked from Britta's office down the long arm of the K-shaped floorplan. He went up two floors to the residential level and walked straight to his room. He sat for a minute in a black-leather barrel chair in the corner of his living area. He was rubbing his temples, collecting his thoughts.

"Screw it," he said, standing up and walking across the room to a heavy, leather messenger bag. It was a primarily a laptop bag, and that was the first thing he threw in. Followed by a couple journals and some scattered manila folders packed full of printed documents.

He walked out the door with the bag slung over his left shoulder, straps hung across his chest with the bag resting against his right hip. Miles didn't notice Beale and another man walking toward his room from the other direction. He had turned to his left and started walking quickly toward a set of concrete stairs halfway down the corridor. Beale and the second man followed at a distance.

"What's *this* all about?" Beale asked himself. His partner simply shrugged silently in response.

* *

"Hello."

It had been nearly 90 minutes since Britta had left the two researchers in the secure Room 4 tucked away in a disused corridor buried inside the walls of Objekt 221—the primary facility of the global corporation Allied Genetics. The facility was known internally as Anvil Canyon, both in reference to a nuclear testing site from the Cold War and the steep drop-off just a quarter mile to the south side of the structure.

Cadey had had her eyes closed, rubbing her temples to relieve the pain and pressure that had built up there. Damon, shockingly, had fallen asleep.

At the sound, both of them snapped alert and turned toward the sound.

"Let's get you out of here," Miles Lofton said, standing in the center of the glass wall, leather bag slung over his shoulder, smile on his face.

* *

"We have a problem," Britta said, hanging up her phone.

She was still in her office. She sat behind her desk and two men sat opposite. Marcus and Carter remained with her after their short meeting nearly 30 minutes ago.

"Another one?" Wittington asked. "Or a different version of the same problem?"

"Another one," she answered. "That was Rico. They now have reports from three satellite facilities. Frenchman's Flat. Hochhaus. Rainier Mesa. Confirmed lost. Complete destruction."

"Oh my God," Marcus said.

"Apparently," she continued, "they enacted Blast Protocol at the Mesa. The data facility at Owl Mountain. However, there was a failure in the system and one room remained untouched."

There was silence around the office.

"Sven Mathias's office, if it matters," she continued. "The company is afraid that a rival has paid a group to data mine against us with a scorched earth policy."

"We're up against a ticking clock," Carter said, standing to go inform his staff.

"Like never before," Britta added, before waving the two men away and answering her ringing phone.

* *

"Fuck you," Damon said.

"Come on," Miles replied. "You gotta trust me. It's time to go. I can get us out."

"I trusted you a week ago. Now? Not so much."

"This company has reached a level of evil that I did not understand," Miles said, moving toward the door. "They're going to kill you. And probably me. We'll all be buried in a shallow grave 100 million years ago to be eaten by Cretaceous worms." He reached up and started pressing buttons on the keypad.

Boom.

Lofton's eyes went wide and his mouth hung open. He was frozen in that position for five seconds. In that time, both Cadey and Damon jumped to their feet and rushed to the window. Suddenly, Miles simply collapsed. He fell straight down and crumpled on the floor just to the right of the door. From his left, into the two captives' field of vision, walked Jason Beale. He was holstering his sidearm. He stood for a moment, looking first at Lofton's corpse and then through the glass at the two prisoners.

He turned to his support man.

"Clean this up," Beale said. "Quietly. Black canvas. Put him in cold storage. Theta Level. Stay out of sight."

"Copy that, sir."

"You two," Beale said, turning his attention back to Damon and Cadey. "Hang out for just a minute more."

He grinned at them and walked away.

CHAPTER FIFTEEN
THE ASSAULT ON ANVIL CANYON

THURSDAY THE 10th started poorly for Objekt 221, the crown jewel of Allied Genetics' facilities. At 4:05 in the morning, every CO2 detector in the building started sounding an alert. At 4:10, every television began showing a digital broadcast of a 45-second loop of cartoon character SpongeBob SquarePants and his nemesis Plankton singing about what it means to have fun. At 4:15, all of the facility's lights flickered off. Anvil Canyon was bathed in the calming green glow of emergency illumination.

"Sweet baby Jesus," Beale said, hopping out of bed.

He keyed the walkie-talkie that sat on his nightstand. The duty chief held the other unit.

"Carson," he said. "What the fuck is going on?"

There was a crackle and a high-pitched whine. Beale was only able to snatch a few words of Carson's response.

"Internal…hack…sent a group…communications blockade…"

With a final pop, the walkie-talkie went dead.

"Christ," Beale said and put it back on the charger.

* *

Five miles away and circling the facility was an E-3G Sentry. It was the "Hammerhead" variant developed in 2015 by Boeing. It was a military aircraft known, largely, for having an enormous radar dish mounted at the rear of the fuselage. Measuring 10 meters in diameter, this technological marvel was responsible for the craft's weather monitoring and threat-detection systems. The Hammerhead variant upped the processing power by several factors to account for the military's increasing battles with cyber terrorists. The Sergott Solutions version contained even more digital tricks.

Jon "Beans" Culver stalked behind the row of 14 computers onboard the E-3G. Everyone was tapping away at their keyboards, calling out notes, time-stamps, and marks against their checklist. Culver's assistant—a fussy civilian with a clipboard—followed him along, making notes and calling orders out.

Their orders were clear: rain a hacker hell down upon Objekt 221 to distract them from the incoming assault force.

* *

Alex Scott and Rick Everson were leading a group of jumpers in a HALO assault. A style of military free-fall, a HALO jump—high altitude, low opening—is a rapid incursion where the paratroopers don't open their parachutes until the last possible moment. It was a precision jump that started 30,000 feet above Anvil Canyon. A force of 20 Wraith soldiers, plus their two commanders, knifed through the cold, dark Crimean air, plummeting toward Objekt 221, a facility in chaos.

* *

At 4:20 in the morning, everyone with an Anvil Canyon email address had a message pop up on whatever device was handy—computer, laptop, tablet, phone—that explained the facility was in the midst of a military training exercise. For their safety, all personnel should exit the building. It looked official, but they had no idea that the email was a complete fabrication.

Security personnel were already in the hallways directing staff-members to a bunker designated Sub One. Britta and Beale stood outside her office door, watching the flow of people heading for the stairs.

"All of the elevators are locked?" she asked.

Beale nodded, just as the song "Afternoon Delight" by Starland Vocal Band erupted over the loudspeakers—punctuated by the shrill CO_2 sensor warning that had been sounding for 20 minutes.

"Lockdown the facility. Get your men to the entrance. We're about to be invaded."

Beale nodded.

"Yes, ma'am," he said and walked away.

* *

Damon Butcher and Cadey Park sat in the conference room chairs, leaned back, feet on the table. They had both slept poorly the previous night and were observing the madness around them with distracted levity. Since they weren't in a high-traffic area, they had only seen a couple people move past them to a staircase at the far end of the corridor. The handful of O221 workers had paid them no mind even as Damon rushed to the wall and knocked on the glass. From that position, he could see just a faint outline of the blood Miles had spilled on the floor hours ago.

Now, they were alone, listening to "Afternoon Delight," trying to remain comfortable.

"I hate this song," Cadey said.

Damon nodded.

"Yeah."

* *

"We are locked as the inbound signal," Jon's assistant was noting, reading off his clipboard. "All outbound signals are completely blocked."

"Good," Jon said. He keyed his microphone that went to all commanders and Clay Reed at the European office. "Remote Mad is a go. Charger and Challenger, cleared for landing."

Alex "Beef" Scott groaned into his throat mic.

* *

As the majority of the Anvil Canyon residents were herded into the lowest protected level of the facility—Sub One—Beale had taken his security force to the main entrance of the building. Britta, for her part, had retreated to her sanctum. For many people, this would have been a personal residence. For her, though, the place where she was most comfortable was her office.

She sat at the giant desk and flipped a small switch hidden on the lip, right at the center of the underside of the desk. This toggle switch caused a large plate to drop out of the bottom of the desk. Britta pulled two custom Sig MPX SBR submachine guns—similar to those favored by the Wraiths—out of the hidden drawer. They were chrome-plated, were fitted with extended magazines, and sported the after-market red-dot sight. She placed the guns on the desk and removed two extra mags for each weapon. Director Vragi sat back in her chair and frowned at the door while SpongeBob SquarePants sang to her from her computer tablet.

"F is for fire that burns down the whole town;

"U is for uranium...BOMBS."

She sighed and flipped the tablet over so the screen was facing down. It did little to quiet the song.

* *

Twenty-two Wraith fighters landed a half-kilometer from the main entrance to Objekt 221. Another 10 men, including force commander Eric "Sixpack" Bilkins, were performing the opposite maneuver as Charger and Challenger—a HAHO, high altitude, high opening parachute insertion. Following the remote hacker disruption and the assault of the advance force, Bilkins and his team would come in undetected to provide support and cleanup.

The advance team disconnected their gear and buried it quickly, leaving their parachutes, harnesses, and oxygen masks in shallow holes—not necessarily for secrecy, more for ease of equipment recovery.

"Let's go," Scott said into his throat mic. "Double-quick."

He glanced at the first hints of the morning sun over the horizon and checked his watch. It was just after 4:20 in the morning. According to Clay's original plan, it should be pure chaos inside the facility.

When the Wraiths, dressed in black with black body armor, made it to the main entrance of Anvil Canyon, they expected heavy resistance. There were two members of the O221 security team stationed behind concrete barriers wielding heavy machine guns. The defensive force was quickly overwhelmed and the Wraiths entered the facility.

It was a madhouse.

Minus people.

The combined Wraith team saw a few stragglers escape down what looked like a stair-head halfway down the corridor. There was a big red sign with white lettering that read Stair E and the door slammed shut.

As the big team passed Stair A and Stair B, they met the second defensive force. It was two daily security personnel commanded by a soldier in black combat gear. The Wraiths opened fire and immediately cut down the three men. The two commanders huddled, three Wraiths facing forward and three facing the rear, all with weapons at the ready.

"I'll take a team and head up to the operations office," Alex "Beef" Scott said, looking from Ahab down to his wrist computer and back up. "Britta Vragi."

Ahab nodded.

"Okay," he said. "I'll take my team and follow *them*." He nodded his head toward the door—Stair E—that they saw the workers escape through.

"It might be a trap," Alex said.

"I'm aware," Rick responded and smiled. The two men bumped fists. "Challenger, mount up."

Rick turned to leave and several Wraith soldiers followed him.

Alex rolled his eyes.

"Jesus Christ," he said. "*Again* with the Team Challenger."

"You know you love it," Ahab said over the team voice channel.

* *

They heard the echo of people running downstairs and the slam of a door.

"Ramirez," Ahab said into this throat mic. "Take point."

One of the Wraith soldiers crept out ahead of the others and slithered down the first few steps. He was leaning over the railing, pointing his weapon around the corner, waiting for any conflict. The stairway, minus Team Challenger, was deserted.

"Clear," Ramirez said.

He started down the stairs, cautiously, with the rest of the team behind him. It was two flights of stairs but only one defined level. They reached the terminal door after a minute.

"Stack up," Ahab said softly to his men. Four soldiers on one side of the door and four on the other. Rick reached for the door's handle and gently slid it to the open position. Ramirez pulled out a small dental appliance—a mirror—and held it through the tiny crack that the opening door created. Ahab held the door open only an inch or so, giving Ramirez a chance to gaze around the area beyond.

"Clear," he said. "Corridor extends to the right and left. Right—large door, closed. Left—corridor terminates in 20 meters. Center—another offshoot corridor. T-junction. All empty."

"Copy that," Ahab said, pulling the door closed. "Weapons free. Ramirez, take your team and secure the large door. Defensive positions. I'll scout the T-junction and firm up."

"Hoorah," Ramirez said.

Ahab pulled open the door.

* *

"Thinkin' of you's workin' up my appetite, looking forward to a little afternoon delight."

The overhead speakers were relentless. Coupled with the CO_2 sensor warning, the sound of the Wraith team's movements were completely masked. Ahab was certain that that door at the end of the corridor was some sort of panic room, likely with monitors directly tied into the facility's surveillance. His team would secure that end of the hall while he took a cautious look down the T-junction.

Everson used a similar mirror to peek down the green corridor. There was a single man, walking away from him. Ahab took a few steps down the hallway. About halfway down, on the right, he could see a glass wall and a solitary door.

"Freeze," Ahab called, gun at the ready. He held his Sig M25 Navy in both hands, trigger discipline, aimed at the enemy's back.

The man, 10 meters away, slowly turned, hands up. The wrist-mounted computer beeped. It was a facial recognition warning. Ahab ignored it for the moment.

"Keep your hands where I can see them," he said. "Walk to me slowly."

The man followed Ahab's orders. He was wearing jeans and a polo shirt. He had a black combat vest on with gear attached to it. He had a pistol in a thigh holster and Velcro name-tape on his chest.

"Jason Beale," Ahab said, reading aloud from the screen on his wrist.

In an instant, Beale jumped forward and knocked the pistol from Ahab's hands. He ducked under a punch and pulled his own pistol out as he slid past the larger Wraith. Their positions reversed, Beale held his own pistol at the ready. Rick "Ahab" Everson held his own hands, palms out, chest high.

"Who the fuck are you?" Beale asked.

"I'm here for the scientists," Ahab said, taking a step closer. They were separated by just over four feet.

"The new guy and that Asian bitch?" Beale said. "You can have 'em." He paused, a wry smile crossed his lips. "You'll never find the others."

In a quick move, Ahab lunged forward. He was a much taller man than Beale and had a greater reach. He knocked the gun away and held Beale's hand in a vice-like grip with his right hand. He let his momentum carry him forward into a vicious head-butt aimed directly at the bridge of Beale's nose. Blood exploded from Beale's face as he dropped immediately to the ground.

Standing over him, Ahab finally looked fully at his screen. *Jason Beale. Army Rangers. Terminal at Major. Commander of Alpha Team— the military wing of the Objekt 221 facility. Considered lethal in armed and unarmed combat.*

"Yeah. Okay," Ahab said and keyed his throat mic.

* *

"We're all five-by," came the voice over Beef's earpiece. It was Ahab checking in. He sounded out of breath, but in control. "Security on the north end is subdued and the scientists have been located in a secure bunker. I will leave a force to maintain position until Sixpack gets here. Taking two men to continue search for HVT. Looks like only two were brought back."

"Copy that," Alex responded. They were still searching for the scientists.

"Sixpack is en route," Jon "Beans" Culver said from his position as airborne overwatch. "Ten minutes out."

"Copy that," Ahab said.

"Copy that," Beef said.

"Overwatch out," Jon said and then clicked off.

* *

Alex continued down the corridor with six men. Their target was the director's office. While the overall priority was the rescue of the scientists named in the death-sentence email, they were still tasked by their contractor to recover crucial data and eliminate certain personnel. Britta Vragi was the name on Alex's list. And the O221 floorplan took up the entirety of his wrist pad—with the path to her office highlighted yellow.

"We go left," he said to his team.

The corridor was still bathed in green from the emergency lighting system. As well as the echo of "Afternoon Delight" masking their footsteps. There was a small star highlighting the office location on their wire-frame map.

Britta Vragi's office was a fortress with one feature—an enormous desk, centrally located. Two of Scott's soldiers breached the door and were immediately pummeled with withering submachine gun fire. The rest of the men backed up to the cover of the hallway. Alex pulled a small cylinder from a Velcro pocket on his thigh. He held it up to his remaining team, activated it, and rolled it into the office.

Britta had anticipated the appearance of the flash-bang grenade and had hidden under her desk, shielding her eyes.

The desk was specially designed from a siege mentality perspective. A combination of heavy steel and reinforced concrete was hiding under the polished adornments and gaudy details. It took Britta weeks to decide what office was going to be hers because she was sure she'd never be able to move it.

Under the desk, she was protected on three sides, and she faced the only opening—which faced the back wall of her office. In the moments while her ears were ringing from the flash grenade, she ejected the two empty clips and reloaded her twin SMGs.

Alex glanced quickly into the office, illuminated by the dull thud of green emergency lighting. He was able to grab the boot of one of his downed Wraiths. He pulled the corpse out of the office.

"She's barricaded under the desk," Alex said to his team. "It looks to be fortified." He paused, thinking. "Three guesses," he said to his men.

"We wait her out," the first soldier said. "Draw her fire. Expend her ammo."

Alex shook his head.

"She could have a crate of mags under there."

"Smoke her out," a second man said. "Lob in two or three smoke grenades. Gas the whole room."

Alex nodded.

"Not bad," he replied. "I can't imagine she has a tactical mask under her desk. But I kind of want to end this quickly. Her office is what we're after."

A third Wraith had been pulling the second lifeless body out of Britta's office.

"Bouncing Betty," he said without turning around.

"Bingo," Alex said, motioning to his grenadier to hand him the item.

Based on the German shrapnel mine of the same name, the Bouncing Betty grenade was ringed with tiny springs. It was designed to hit the ground and launch itself three feet into the air before detonation.

"Half pocket, off the rail," Alex said as he tossed the grenade into the office. He overshot the huge desk in an arc. The grenade hit the back wall and the spring liner ejected the explosive back into the room—right toward the one weakness in Britta's desk, the back opening.

"Aw, fuck me..." Britta said, closing her eyes.

Boom.

"Clear out what you can," Alex said, standing. "Continue to sweep. I'm going to rendezvous with Ahab and locate our remaining HVTs."

"Copy that," the soldiers responded before piling into the smoking office.

CHAPTER SIXTEEN
THE ESCAPE IN THE DEAD OF MORNING

THEY HEARD gunshots. There was an echo of the shots themselves, the ricochet off metal, and, occasionally, a groan. Damon and Cadey both looked up from their silent reverie at the same time. "Afternoon Delight" had looped three or four times and the two were content with sitting in their moderately comfortable conference room chairs. As the previous night had worn on, they both became increasingly emotional about their predicament. First, after seeing Miles Lofton gunned down right in front of them, they were depressed at what seemed like a similar fate. As the hours drug on, though, they became mad. Resentful. Angered that the company had not only made this horrifying decision, but was now content with making them wait.

And not wait in their own assigned residences, but a secret conference room that obviously pulled double-duty as a hidden meeting room and a space to stash potentially unruly prisoners.

Eventually, their fatigue overwhelmed them.

They were rudely awoken with most of the rest of the facility with the initial CO2 alarm. It was only compounded with the hazard lighting and, now, the hypnotic, if unpleasant, melodies of the Starland Vocal Band.

They looked up and then stood up in unison.

"Gunshots," Damon said.

"Seriously?" Cadey asked. She had escaped North Korea in her youth, but had never been shot at outside a videogame. Damon, however, had spent many years in the Marines, retiring as a force recon commando. "Are you sure?"

He cocked an eyebrow, looking at the HVAC system as if that would somehow focus his hearing, where the echoes were coming from.

"Pretty sure."

He started to pace around the room.

"I think this facility is under attack," he finally said, turning back to Cadey, who still stood listening to the sounds. She turned to him.

"From who?"

Damon shrugged.

"I'm not sure I want to find out," he said. "It feels like our fates are sealed, and I doubt these people care much about us. We might be going from the frying pan into the fire with a hostile takeover."

Cadey paused, pursing her eyebrows.

"What could be worse than being shot by that asshole Beale?"

Damon was looking around the room. He walked to the section of wall that framed the door.

"Torture, maybe," he said. "Watching our friends and family being tortured. Forced servitude. Information extraction. Scientific experiments."

"Okay, okay, fine," she said, and paused. "What are you doing?"

He was knocking on the wall around the door.

"What do you think?" he said. "Concrete? Or drywall? It sounds like drywall."

There was a three-foot section of wall between the door and where the glass partition took over.

"I think it's drywall and they're too busy upstairs to pay any attention to us." He paused for a moment. "Reinforced drywall? Sheetrock?"

He turned and grabbed one of the chairs. Damon grunted as he whipped the chair through the air and smashed it into the section of wall near the door. It was a dull sound, but encouraging. He smiled at Cadey, who smiled back.

Again, again, again.

He smashed the chair into the wall half a dozen times, until the armrest was bent and two of the rollers had broken off. The wall, though, was severely damaged.

"Yes," Cadey said, smiling.

They started pulling chunks out, punching and kicking the wall. Soon, they had broken off enough to not only see the studs that supported this section of wall and door frame, but the back side of the security panel.

"Bingo," Damon said.

"Do you think shorting it out will get us out of here?"

Damon looked over at her and smiled.

"I suppose," he said. "I was planning on kicking my way through the other side."

* *

They stood in the hallway—free in the micro, but not the macro. They had made a mess and didn't bother to clean it up. The green glow of the emergency lighting lit their way down the corridor. The LED bulbs were spaced every 10 yards or so and offered enough illumination to keep them going. The magnetic locks on the stairwell doors had automatically disengaged when the main power was shut down.

"This way," Cadey said, turning right and running down the corridor.

* *

Madness.

The sign above the door said Stair 3C, but neither of them actually knew what that meant. They soon found out that the conference room floor was only one level beneath the main area of O221. They exited the stairs slowly, pushing open the door with no sudden movements. The gunfire in this area of the facility had stopped.

"Shit," Cadey said, under her breath, but loud enough for Damon to hear it.

Open just six inches, they could see that the main corridor—the big vertical in the capital K that was their floorplan—was abandoned, save for three dead security agents that they could immediately see. Two were dressed in standard-issue khaki pants and dark blue polo shirts, emblazoned with the Allied Genetics logo over the left chest. The third, however, was dressed more like a soldier. He wore the black combat gear that Beale and his men had worn just hours ago when apprehending Damon and the other researchers.

The two snuck out into the corridor and pulled whatever gear they could off the dead men.

"Gross," Cadey said, taking a pistol and a cell phone off the least-disgusting of the two security men. Damon showed no remorse or fear in rifling through the dead soldier's gear. He had a neat bullet hole through the center of his forehead, and his eyes stared at the ceiling.

Damon wrestled with the corpse for a tense moment as he pulled the combat vest off and then wrenched the Glock 19 pistol from the man's right hand. Damon put on the vest and checked the chamber of the weapon. He had three spare magazines along the sides of his new gear.

He stood and peered down one end of the hall, turned, and looked down the other side.

"Is there anything in your room...?" he started.

Cadey shook her head.

"Nothing that can't be replaced," she said. "Let's get out of here."

Damon nodded. They turned toward the main entrance of the facility and jogged away from the 3C door.

* *

Just outside the building, they saw two more dead men. It looked like they were the first line of defense. Their corpses were draped over two concrete barriers that were at once decorative and destructive. Damon remembered them from first coming to the Anvil Canyon facility. They reminded him of a relic of the Cold War—huge, thick, sturdy, and built to stop a tank. The Allied Genetics logo had been artfully carved into them with a year that probably represented the company's incorporation. Even with all of this decoration, the tank traps remained imposing.

Cadey and Damon skirted the two and jogged outside into the cool morning air.

"Hey, hold up," came a voice from behind them.

They stopped, guns up.

"Hey, whoa, that's not necessary," the man said.

Damon squinted. Cadey quietly snarled, clearly lumping him in amongst the group of people who wanted her dead.

"Marcus Osborne," she said under her breath to Damon.

"Head of Personnel," Damon finished for her.

Marcus had come out the same door they had just exited. He stood in the middle of no-man's land—20 meters from the door, and 20 meters from the two researchers.

"I'm unarmed," Marcus said, raising his hands. He turned his hands forward and backward to further solidify that he wasn't a threat. Damon saw the black smudge that he recognized as a tattoo on the man's right hand. While he couldn't see it in any great detail from that distance, Damon remembered it to be a black scorpion.

"The darker the color, the more dangerous the venom," Damon said to himself. He started to lower his Glock, and Cadey did the same with hers.

"What happened in there, Marcus?" Cadey called in a neutral tone, purely on a fact-finding mission.

Marcus began lowering his hands also. He started walking toward the two researchers, but something was wrong. It was a halted gait. He looked, to Damon, as if he was doing math in his head while attempting to walk normally.

"I don't know," he called across the shortening expanse. "I was going to ask you guys."

Marcus had slowly cut the distance in half and now stopped.

"My God," he said. "What time is it?"

He made a big show of putting his hands on his hips and stretching his back. Marcus scratched his side with his right hand and continued the scratch around his back. Damon thumbed off the safety catch on his pistol. With a jerk, Marcus brought his right hand back out around his side, holding a black pistol.

Damon had been waiting for this and shot Marcus in the face. In fact, there were two shots.

"Shit," Cadey said.

They looked around for where the second shot had come from.

"The darker the what?" she said, still looking.

"Homespun wisdom," Damon said, turning to his right, gun still raised. "The color of a scorpion. The darker the color, the more venomous he is. I spent some time in the desert."

"That's right," came a new voice from behind Marcus.

While similar, his gear was different, more streamlined, than the O221 soldiers. He walked toward them in an easy gait. He held his hands up, his own pistol—smoking barrel—was hung by the trigger finger of his right hand.

"Damon Butcher, Cadey Park," he said. "I'm Alex Scott. I represent Sergott Solutions. We were hired by Precision Robotics to rescue you."

"I wonder if they're still hiring," Cadey said, smiling.

For his part, Damon simply smiled and exhaled.

CHAPTER SEVENTEEN
THE NUCLEAR OPTION

"BEST I can figure, that area was historically known to have strange properties." Weeks later, Damon Butcher sat in the same Precision Robotics lunchroom where he had first been approached by Marcus Osborne. He was eating lunch with a recently hired Cadey Park. And they had worked to fill in the missing pieces of their Allied Genetics adventure. "There are accounts of people going missing dating back several hundred years. They probably hit a soft spot and got shot back into the Cretaceous Era. Only to get eaten by a dinosaur."

Cadey nodded. She was finishing up her lunch by working through a small bag of baby-cut carrots.

"I know some of the data-miners here," she said, chewing on one side of her mouth to speak freely. "Your buddy Jeff, for one. Allied was planning some pretty far-out stuff. Gene modification. Splices. Hybrids. Armor. Even the plants they were assigning us to bring back. They could be made into fairly toxic combinations."

Damon nodded in turn.

He leaned in a bit closer to her and dropped his voice a bit.

"That's the problem, right?"

Cadey cocked an eyebrow.

"The next step. Escalation," Damon said. "Presumably, Precision wanted to disrupt or shut down Allied's operations—and they did—but, what do they do now?" He wadded up his napkin and tossed it into the brown paper bag that served as their trash can on the table. "Did they destroy all the facilities? Will they destroy all the research?"

"Or will they find a nice insertion point and continue where Allied left off?" Cadey offered. "I don't know of any competitors," she continued. "Not directly, at least. Precision could start with the research that's been done and make huge strides in many areas."

They were silent for a moment, swiftly clearing the small table of their respective lunches. Finally, Damon shrugged.

"I guess we'll just have to be ready to intervene," he said.

"Damn right," Cadey said, smiling.

AFTERWORD
THE END OF THE END

I FIND all elements of the creative process fascinating – from the initial planning stage to revising the final version. Every story has a story, completely unique from anything else a writer has worked on. This story is no different.

It's a 12-hour road trip from Toledo, Ohio, to Minneapolis, Minnesota. While making this trek in June of 2017, I let my mind wander and ended up plotting Pandemic (a story about a terrorist hacker group who figures out a way to program computer viruses that would also target humans) and Objekt 221. The plot for O221 felt the most complete so I decided to write it first.

Here you go.

I'm a huge fan of the television program "Mysteries of the Abandoned" where they find bizarre structures that seem to have no purpose and explore either in person or through data mining the structure's origins. And, of course, unravel the mystery of why it was abandoned. It seems like 9 times out of 10, the facility was originally built as a military installation. Even though it's a fairly common "twist," I'm endlessly entertained. So, it was fun to explore some of these locations on my own. Only one of the military locations in this story is a complete fabrication …

Additionally, the idea of a super-ancient civilization has always been intriguing. Even though it only amounts to a footnote in this story, the existence of The Road and Building 5 were great fun to conceptualize and write about.

What fun it was to blend all of these ideas together into the same story!

I hope you had a good time flipping through this one, kind reader. It felt like a quick-moving story even with the intentionally slowed-down bits (discussion about the uncanny valley, for example, or the mysterious basement computer at Michigan State University).

Objekt 221 (simply referred to as *Dino* during the writing process) was somewhat delayed because I paused in its writing to put together the second Event short story collection. But the story never strayed far from my fingertips, and I was happy to finally let it reach its conclusion.

Enjoy the story … I certainly have. If you want to talk about it, you can find me at many of the finer social media outlets or at the website www.steve-metcalf.com.

Keep reading. Keep writing.

Steve Metcalf
May 23rd, 2019
New Hope, Minnesota

CHECK OUT OTHER GREAT DINOSAUR BOOKS

PRIMORDIA
by **Greig Beck**

Ben Cartwright, former soldier, home to mourn the loss of his father stumbles upon cryptic letters from the past between the author, Arthur Conan Doyle and his great, great grandfather who vanished while exploring the Amazon jungle in 1908.

Amazingly, these letters lead Ben to believe that his ancestor's expedition was the basis for Doyle's fantastical tale of a lost world inhabited by long extinct creatures. As Ben digs some more he finds clues to the whereabouts of a lost notebook that might contain a map to a place that is home to creatures that would rewrite everything known about history, biology and evolution.

But other parties now know about the notebook, and will do anything to obtain it. For Ben and his friends, it becomes a race against time and against ruthless rivals.

In the remotest corners of Venezuela, along winding river trails known only to lost tribes, and through near impenetrable jungle, Ben and his novice team find a forbidden place more terrifying and dangerous than anything they could ever have imagined.

PANGAEA EXILES
by **Jeff Brackett**

Tried and convicted for his crimes, Sean Barrow is sent into temporal exile—banished to a time so far before recorded history that there is no chance that he, or any other criminal sent back, has any chance of altering history.

Now Sean must find a way to survive more than 200 million years in the past, in a world populated by monstrous creatures that would rend him limb from limb if they got the chance. And that's just his fellow prisoners.

The dinosaurs are almost as bad.

CHECK OUT OTHER GREAT DINOSAUR BOOKS

FLIPSIDE
by JAKE BIBLE

The year is 2046 and dinosaurs are real.

Time bubbles across the world, many as large as one hundred square miles, turn like clockwork, revealing prehistoric landscapes from the Cretaceous Period.

They reveal the Flipside.

Now, thirty years after the first Turn, the clockwork is breaking down as one of the world's powers has decided to exploit the phenomenon for their own gain, possibly destroying everything then and now in the process.

A MAN OUT OF TIME
by Christopher Laflan

Five years after the Chinese Axis detonated an unknown weapon of mass destruction off the southern coast of the United States, Special Ops Sergeant John Crider and the members of Shadow Company have finally captured what they all hope will lead to the end of the war. Unfortunately, the population within the United States is no longer sustainable. In an effort to stabilize the economy, the government enacts the Cryonics Act. One hundred years in suspended animation, all debt forgiven, and a chance at a less crowded future are too good to pass up for John and his young daughter.

Except not everything always goes as planned as Sergeant John Crider finds himself pitted against a land of prehistoric monsters genetically resurrected from the fossil record, murderous inhabitants, and a future he never wanted.

CHECK OUT OTHER GREAT DINOSAUR BOOKS

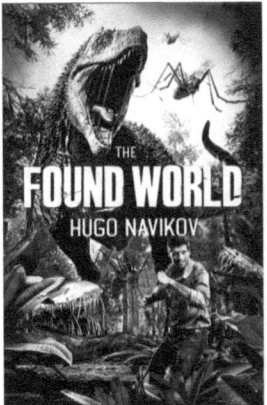

THE FOUND WORLD
by **Hugo Navikov**

A powerful global cabal wants adventurer Brett Russell to retrieve a superweapon stolen by the scientist who built it. To entice him to travel underneath one of the most dangerous volcanoes on Earth to find the scientist, this shadowy organization will pay him the only thing he cares about: information that will allow him to avenge his family's murder.

But before he can get paid, he and his team must enter an underground hellscape of killer plants, giant insects, terrifying dinosaurs, and an army of other predators never previously seen by man.

At the end of this journey awaits a revelation that could alter the fate of mankind ... if they can make it back from this horrifying found world.

HOUSE OF THE GODS
by **Davide Mana**

High above the steamy jungle of the Amazon basin, rise the flat plateaus known as the Tepui, the House of the Gods. Lost worlds of unknown beauty, a naturalistic wonder, each an ecology onto itself, shunned by the local tribes for centuries. The House of the Gods was not made for men.

But now, the crew and passengers of a small charter plane are about to find what was hidden for sixty million years.

Lost on an island in the clouds 10.000 feet above the jungle, surrounded by dinosaurs, hunted by mysterious mercenaries, the survivors of Sligo Air flight 001 will quickly learn the only rule of life on Earth: Extinction.